Praise for
Richard Godwin

"A tense slice of international Noir that oozes atmosphere."

    —**Paul D Brazill,** author of *Guns of Brixton* and *A Case of Noir*

"Once more Richard Godwin proves he is the only worthy successor to Patricia Highsmith. His Novel is a deliciously tantalizing bit of dark psychological thriller that will make you think twice about whom you make friends with while on vacation. You won't want to put this one down for a second."

    —**Vincent Zandri,** NY Times and USA Today best-selling author of *Everything Burns and Moonlight Weeps*

"Richard Godwin does it again! With the adroit skill of a seasoned writer that knows that human decency is just a fragile scab on a wound that harbors a violent world seething in sex, drugs, lust and death.

    —**Lou Boxer,** Founder of *NoirCon*

"Only Godwin. It's a phrase you'll use often when you get acquainted with the sensual and sultry atmosphere of this master storyteller. This is some of his most accessible work, but it's one of his most textured and refined as well. Only Godwin can pull it off every time like that."

    —**Benoît Lelièvre,** *deadendfollies.com*

"Claude meets Maxine knee-deep in the Caribbean and knows he'd do anything to make her his: anything. But keeping her means raising the stakes: cash, guns, gangsters and a return to his bad old habits. Will there be enough of him left to keep her by the time he's through? Godwin makes his Narrative lethally sexy—which makes this story just right."

—**K.A. Laity,** author of *White Rabbit*

"Don Juan meets the Marquis de Sade meets Kafka meets Jim Thompson meets Richard Godwin who gets them all together in one room and they collaborate. It's a brilliant success."

—**Les Edgerton,** author of *The Genuine, Imitation, Plastic Kidnapping, The Bitch, The Rapist* and others

"With extraordinary writing, characterization, and storytelling, Godwin is truly one of our great writers."

—**Luca Veste,** author of *Dead Gone*

Also by
Richard Godwin

Apostle Rising

Mr Glamour

One Lost Summer

Meaningful Conversations

Paranoia And The Destiny Programme

Noir City

ABOUT THE AUTHOR

Richard Godwin is the critically acclaimed author of *Apostle Rising, Mr. Glamour, One Lost Summer, Noir City, Meaningful Conversations, Confessions Of A Hit Man, Paranoia And The Destiny Programme, Wrong Crowd, Savage Highway, Ersatz World, The Pure And The Hated, Disembodied, Buffalo And Sour Mash, Locked In Cages* and *Crystal On Electric Acetate.*

His stories have been published in numerous paying magazines and over 34 anthologies, among them an anthology of his stories, *Piquant: Tales Of The Mustard Man, The Mammoth Book Of Best British Crime* and *The Mammoth Book Of Best British Mystery,* alongside Lee Child.

He was born in London and lectured in English and American literature at the University of London. He also teaches creative writing at University and workshops. You can find out more about him at his website **www.richardgodwin.net**, where you can read a full list of his works, and where you can also read his Chin Wags At The Slaughterhouse, his highly popular and unusual interviews with other authors.

TWISTED LOVE

by

RICHARD GODWIN

This paperback edition published in Great Britain in 2018 by
Black Jackal Books, Suite 106, 143 Kingston Road, London SW19 1LJ

ISBN: 978-1-9997858-3-3

Book layout by Guido Henkel
Cover design by Lieu Pham, Covertopia.com

Papers used by Black Jackal Books are natural renewable and recyclable products sourced from well-managed forests and certified in accordance with the rules of the Forest Stewardship Council.

Printed by ImprintDigital.com, Exeter, United Kingdom

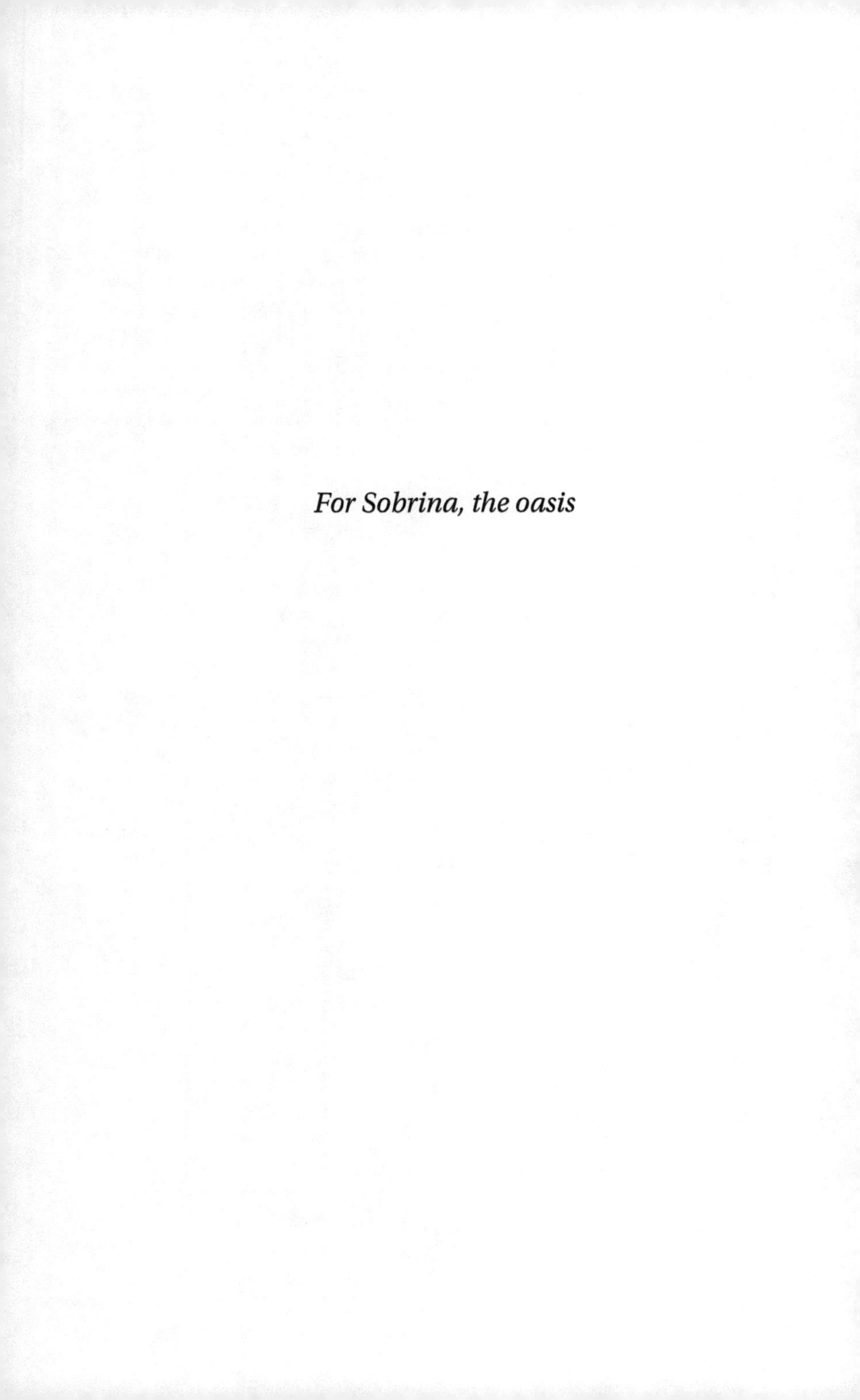

For Sobrina, the oasis

1

SEDUCTIONS IN BARS, FAST CARS, LOOSE WOMEN, ALL THOSE beautiful young things waiting for it to happen, and it did, all the way form the Caribbean to London.

#

Claude was knee-deep in the blue water of the Caribbean Sea when he first saw Maxine. Drops of sea water were running off her brown shoulders and she seemed to stop time with an appeal that was infinite. That day beneath an intense indigo sky he made eye contact with her as she got out of the water and walked over to the bar. He would later look back on it as a defining moment, one of those rare events in a person's life when they are offered something they've secretly desired but never believed they're capable of having. There were few things in life that Claude really wanted, but she was one of them. And he knew it instantly. He often wondered, after it all happened, if he hadn't been drunk on Pina coladas, whether he would have made the first move and she would have vanished from his life like so many chances he'd let slip.

As it was, he stood up, walked over to her and, holding up his glass, said, 'Can I get you one?'

Maxine didn't say anything for a few seconds, just held him in her steady gaze that gave nothing away, and Claude begin to shrink inside his own skin, about to walk away.

'Sure,' she said, a sparkle in her deep brown eyes.

She was looking at him over the rims of her shades, and Claude found it sexy, the way she was taking him in.

He came back from the bar with two chilled coladas which they sat sipping beneath a parasol that advertised boating trips. And he felt someone had pierced his heart with a small fish hook.

He looked at her, at her inviting skin, the curve of her body in her swim suit, and said, 'Are you here alone?'

'My friend went into town.'

He nodded.

'Friend.'

That night he took her out.

Her friend, Doris, was an overweight blonde who laughed nervously when she spoke. Claude met her briefly, maybe for two minutes at the Montehabana hotel where Maxine was staying. Doris offered Claude her cheek and he smelt vodka on her breath. They left her nursing a hangover and went out to eat at Dune's.

'I heard this is the most cutting edge place to eat round here,' Claude said, watching Maxine raise a forkful of swordfish to her moist mouth.

'This is good, oh, yeah,' she said.

He liked the way she lingered over her words, speaking them slowly, as if she was tasting them. He liked the look of her manicured nails on the starched white tablecloth. He liked her perfume, and her Gucci shades, her sensuous hands, and the way her hair touched her shoulders. She seemed immersed in an endless sensual experience he wanted to be part of, as inviting as the blue water outside the restaurant window. He didn't ask her if she had a man, he didn't want the dream to end. They had lime sorbet and cognacs and they sat beneath a sky strewn with stars that Claude felt were placed there especially for them.

'Are you from London?' he said.

'I am.'

'Whereabouts?'

'Hammersmith. And you?'

'Fulham.'

'Just up the road.'

'It feels so far away.'

'Out here, yes.'

They stood by the sea drinking in the salt air, and he was high on the illusion of night. She looked immaculate in an off the shoulder dress, all white, figure hugging, and she made him feel important and wealthy. She was the kind of brunette he used to crave in his marriage, dark hair that shone, dark eyes, a full mouth and figure.

The mood was broken momentarily when she said, 'What do you do?'

He looked away, towards the blurred shore around the bay. A yacht was making its way over the smooth blue water, and music floated through the dark air. It could have been in the middle of the ocean. The horizon of the land was fading in the night.

'I sell boats.'

She took his arm and they walked along the edge of the water. When he kissed her she smelled of peaches and honey.

Claude wanted her, he wanted her like he'd wanted nothing in his life.

'Do you think Doris will mind if you don't go back tonight?'

'She's probably taken a sleeping pill. Where are you staying?'

'The Raquel Boutique.'

And for one night in the tropical heat Claude forgot who he was. Back at his hotel room, with iced wine on the side, he peeled away Maxine's skin tight dress and ran his hand down her arm to her waist.

'You look like a model.'

She wrapped her long arms around his shoulders and stepped out of her stilettos.

'You like me, Claude?'

'I do baby, oh I do.'

'You like high maintenance women?'

He didn't listen to the question because he didn't care any more after she touched him. She stepped out of the dress and stood there with nothing on.

'You see I came prepared,' she said.

'You sure did, what a body.'

She was the greatest high he'd ever known. They slept in his bed as the fevered percussion of crickets filled the erotic night with their incessant rhythm.

2

—————————————————

BUT WHEN HE AWOKE THE NEXT MORNING HE WAS HIMSELF again.

Claude stood in front of the mirror in the hotel he could no longer afford, and turned away. He looked at his heels on the floor next to Maxine's and saw they were almost as long. He looked at his face, and told himself he wasn't bad-looking. With his blue eyes and smile he could charm women, but it was his height that always got in the way for him, and in the past he overcompensated by acting tough. He'd dropped that a while back.

He measured himself against the clean bathroom tiles, pushing out his chest and standing tall, telling himself he was nothing more than a short-arsed loser whose wife left him. He'd got home to a note that read, 'Had enough'. Yvonne had left her keys and wedding ring on the table in the hall. He'd pawned it for beer, which he proceeded to drink over the following week while he ignored all the reasons his marriage had failed. And he knew that he'd always wanted more than what Yvonne offered him. He didn't feel guilty, just acutely aware of the passage of time. He became afraid that one day he'd wake up too old to dream. And so he booked the holiday in Cuba, thinking maybe he'd never return.

Now he stood there in the bathroom thinking how he hated his name. His mother had been a French model whose love of romance had unsettled the working class family he'd been born into. She talked of bohemian artists and lovers, of seductions in exotic settings, wearing revealing clothes that confused Claude and his brother. His father retreated into angry silences and alcohol. It was his mother who had named him. Claude later discovered she had a lover years ago called Claude. When she took her own life his father followed soon after, a morose man Claude watched shrink into liver cancer and amnesia. He'd often wondered if he felt betrayed by his mother's deeds. But he could never determine if his name was a compliment or a test.

He peered out of the bathroom at Maxine. She was sleeping on her stomach, the sheets thrown back. The sight of her naked back and buttocks took his breath away. He wondered if she would put in a bill for the pleasure she'd given him, send him home with a memory and a dose of embarrassment, the experience locked inside him like a dirty secret he couldn't share with friends. He'd had hookers before, but none like her, she didn't act like one. He considered paying for the room and leaving when Maxine awoke. And he reprimanded himself for his inherent cynicism. But when he went into the room she reached out a hand and pulled him back into bed and he thought of more lies, hearing the sound of calypso music outside, wondering what it cost to set up a company that sold boats.

'I can look after you,' he whispered in her ear as she wrapped her thighs round him.

He traced her body into his mind and told himself she wouldn't fade. He watched her shut her eyes and he said, 'I'm done with memories and snapshots.'

They slept late that morning and Claude dreamt he was riding a surfboard on an endless wave. When he awoke he looked out of the window at the sea and the horizon as Maxine showered. He could see her through the open bathroom door. She had the kind of body that belonged in the realm of fantasy, with her full breasts, and endless curves. And he wondered how her body would look in his house. She loved the hotel. She made Claude feel rich.

She went to see how Doris was and met him for lunch at Rio Mar down by the beach.

She wore a blue sarong and drank a Mojito while Claude read the list of cocktails.

'There's one here called a panty dropper,' he said.

It was as she laughed that he decided what he was going to do. He looked at her perfect white teeth and listened to the soft hiss of waves. They reminded him of the way Maxine sighed when he made love to her. They ate surf 'n turf. Claude watched her throat flex and relax as she swallowed.

'I have to go back tomorrow,' he said. 'I'd like to continue this when you return.'

'I'd like that,' she said.

And he felt hungry and alone and high on her. He wanted to be able to afford her, and as he sat there he began to like his name. He realised his mother had given him a test, a signal from a romantic of what life could be. And it all became clear to him beneath the unreal Caribbean sky, as he looked at Maxine, the living fantasy who'd emerged from the waves with all his dreams alive in her hands. She couldn't drop them now. As he craved her, Claude suddenly felt as fragile as a shard that was missing from a stained glass window.

3

CLAUDE RETURNED TO HIS HOUSE ON THE EDGE OF FULHAM, where crumbling Victorian facades bled into the less salubrious quarters of Earl's Court, with its lines of Aussie pubs and tourists stepping out of the underground casting looks over their shoulders and at maps. His was a sleazy neighbourhood seeking an identity among the wealthy. It made him feel cheep and lonely and too old for Maxine, who lingered for a day or two on his collar like a spray of perfume. She was fading from his mind as he relived his night with her. And he wandered the dark hallway of the home he'd shared with his vanished wife and thought of ways of keeping the dream alive.

One morning when he felt Maxine was becoming a fantasy he stared at himself for an hour in the mirror in his bathroom, looking at how middle-aged he'd become without even noticing. And he decided he would try to reclaim Maxine like an ornament from a dive.

He didn't expect the call. He was sitting in his boxer shorts drinking Heineken one weekend when his mobile rang.

'Remember me?' she said, blasting sunlight into his head, as he stared out of the window at the rainswept street, seeing the beach and her body.

'Maxine?'

He ran a hand through his uncombed hair.

'The very same. I'm back in London.'

'That's great. Shall we meet?'

'Hm. I'll have to check my diary.'

He could hear laughter in her voice.

'Well, when you have a moment,' he said.

'I'm teasing, silly.'

#

He met her at Chez Patrick in Kensington, and she looked every bit as desirable as when he'd left her. And Claude wondered why she'd chosen him, with his heels and his middle age.

Afterwards they went to her flat and he took in the sense of her life, a collage of femininity and style. There were no signs of a man or a flat mate. The living room was filled with designer brochures and soft furnishings that came straight from a lifestyle magazine.

He was sipping a Bacardi when she unbuttoned the tie he'd bought at Moss Bros. He'd studied it for hours against the shirt he'd picked for their date. And it all seemed too real and far from the Bahamas and the lies he'd bought her with. Her hand felt smooth on his chest as he unhooked her bra and entered the moonlight again where they strolled on a beach beneath a foreign sun.

They were lying in her bed when he said it.

'So there's no man in your life?'

'Only you.'

It sounded like a song the way she said it and he stared at the Modigliani print she had on the wall opposite the tangled bedclothes and their entwined bodies reflecting in the glass.

'You're a stunning woman, there must be loads of men interested in you.'

She leant on an elbow and looked at him.

'There are. But I'm interested in you.'

He wanted to ask why, but he didn't. Instead he made love to her again, hungrily, desperately, hoping it would never end. As she opened her mouth and moaned he knew that danger tasted better than safety.

He wondered what she would think of his place, and over the ensuing weeks he thought of ways of avoiding taking her there. He hired a team of builders to redecorate and made excuses, until one weekend he couldn't get through to her.

4

THERE WAS ANOTHER MAN AND HIS MAN WAS BERTRAND. He was tall, lean, dark and handsome. The kind of guy Claude thought could pull just about any woman he set his mind to. He had this air of sophistication about him that made Claude feel small and cheap. It was in his movements, the way he used his hands as he talked, and Claude hated him on sight. He followed Maxine, watched her walk arm in arm with him to a French restaurant.

'So why didn't you tell me?' he said when he went to her flat a few days later.

'Were you following me?'

'I drove past, I saw you.'

'Bertrand wasn't part of my life any more when I met you.'

'And now?'

'You kept me away from your house Claude, I'm not stupid.'

'It's not what you think.'

'You're married.'

'No, I'm not married.'

'So why won't you let me go and see where you live?'

'I have a relative. I didn't want you to think I'm encumbered.'

'A relative? Who?'

'My brother. I have to help him out, he was staying with me, he's not now, I felt my lifestyle would put you off.'

'That wouldn't put me off.'

'Then come to my place.'

She poured them both a Pina colada.

'Remember these?'

'How could I forget?'

'Claude, I'm not interested in playing around.'

'What about Bertrand? I saw you with him.'

'He belongs in the past.'

'What about me?'

'You belong in the future.'

'I want you Maxine, I don't want other men around.'

'There are no other men,' she said. 'You really weren't following me?'

'No.'

'I didn't think you had a car.'

'Why did you think that?'

'We always go everywhere in taxis.'

'That's because it's impossible parking in London. I got a car.'

'What is it? Let me guess.'

'A Merc,' he said, before she could put him in a corner.

All through dinner he thought she was lying. They made love back at her flat and he searched her body for physical deception. She looked so beautiful when she came. He put his ear next to her mouth as she did and tasted the sound of her pleasure. He watched her sleeping and wondered what her dreams were. He wanted Bertrand removed. The old Claude would have walked away, the old Claude would never have pulled her. The Claude he found in Cuba thought of guns and violence now, aroused at her naked body as she slept, the sheets thrown back, the light from the streetlamp shining on her full breasts. He touched Maxine in her sleep, running his hand along the contour of her spine, feeling the softness of her body. She could come and live with him where he could watch her all the time. When he was with her he didn't feel like Claude. He wanted to realise the extravagant promise he'd found beneath the Caribbean sun.

5

Bertrand's eyes sparkled when he spoke. He wore long coats that gave him a mysterious air. His aftershave lingered in the air when he walked down the street. The smell nauseated Claude as he followed him. When Maxine agreed to move in she made a request.

'I want to meet your brother, I don't want you hiding anything from me and I won't hide anything from you, OK?'

'Yes,' he said, watching as she slipped out of her clothes, threw her bra on the chair, slid down her G-string and walked about her flat getting changed to go out for supper. Her breasts were as firm as a twenty year old's. Maxine was thirty and she'd told Claude her insecurities about her age. And now he wondered what her body would look like in his house. It was as if her attractiveness was framed by circumstance, and Claude feared he would show up the things she was hiding, as if there was another Maxine.

'I know in a few years men will be looking at younger women, I want to settle down with you,' she said.

He wanted to believe her but couldn't. Not with Bertrand around.

As he watched her get dressed, his arousal at her nudity was soiled by the dirty thought of another man inside her. She must have slept with Bertrand that weekend he couldn't get hold of her. He would ensure Bertrand was nothing more than a memory to her.

He followed him for days, watching the places he went to eat, the women he met. He measured the danger he presented. He knew he wasn't seeing Maxine, but he was there in the background like a bad odour. Bertrand was the kind of man Claude hated, confident with women, at ease. He made them laugh. He knew things Claude didn't, female things. Claude wondered what he knew about Maxine. He thought about hiring a detective to follow him, but he didn't want anyone else knowing.

One day he passed Bertrand in the street. His head came to Bertrand's shoulders and Claude felt like hitting him. Instead he went home and called Spike.

6

Al waited for them at the wine bar Bistro Monte in Fulham. He was nervous, out of place, and sat there looking at the chandeliers and exposed brickwork, wondering what his brother was doing going to a place like this. He looked at the drinks list, at the alien cocktails, and the dance floor, and saw Claude in the mirrored ceiling as he walked in.

His brother was with this bombshell of a woman on his arm, and Al wondered how much he was paying her. She was dressed in a tight blue satin skirt, and a low top that pushed her cleavage up. She moved in a way that made Al feel aroused and uncomfortable, and he looked away from her to Claude. He said nothing as she laid this teeny bag down on the bar and held out her hand.

'Al, this is Maxine,' Claude said.

Al held her hand and kept his eyes on her face, wanting to drop them to her cleavage, feeling Claude's eyes on him.

'I've heard a lot about you, Al.'

'I'm sure.'

'What's that supposed to mean?' Claude said, slapping him on the back as Maxine took in the brother Claude had hidden from her.

His shoes were covered in mud and he looked out of place. Maxine glanced at his waist, wondered how much he weighed, this overweight brother of Claude's. He had a nice face, a face she thought she could trust. He didn't have Claude's eyes. Claude had great eyes, they were the reason she accepted the Pina colada from him when he approached her at the bar as she sat there reassessing her life. Al's eyes had something there she couldn't define, a touch of danger maybe. His hands were heavy, and beneath the flab there was muscle, as if he was out of shape but had once worked out.

Claude ordered a bottle of Burgundy, and listened as his brother talked nervously to Maxine, and sipped without enjoyment from his glass.

'So what do you do?' she said.

Al looked away, at two young women who were laughing at the next table. They were cheap and compromised and the sort of birds he was used to seeing with Claude.

'I'm a van driver.'

'My brother doesn't say much, never did even as a kid,' Claude said. 'Still, you can trust him, can't you, Al?'

Maxine watched Claude squeeze his brother's shoulder, and took in the crumpled mark he left on his shirt.

'So did your mother give a French name too?' Maxine said as they ate some tapas.

'Yeah, Al's short for Alain.'

'I like that, why don't you use it?'

'Where I grew up they'd have taken the piss. I ain't French anyway.'

'Claude stuck with his.'

'He didn't have much choice, what could he shorten it to?'

'It means persevering in Latin,' Claude said, straightening up in his chair as Al chewed on some chorizo.

Maxine leant across the table and picked up a green olive. Claude loved the way she put it in her mouth, the way she ate.

They said their goodbyes outside. Claude watched Al walk away in the rain, head down, as he sheltered Maxine under his umbrella. He returned to her flat and made love to her, seeing Bertrand's face sinking like a shaped dissolving in water. He wanted more from Maxine, more of her body and the things she thought about, he wanted her secret sexual self, the one she shared with other men, he wanted her in ways he'd never wanted anyone before and he smelt gun smoke as he came and felt her clench hard around his throbbing cock.

Afterwards he nodded at himself in the bathroom mirror.

'I'll ask him to do it,' he said.

When he came out, Maxine was making coffee in the kitchen, in a pair of shorts and nothing else.

'Your brother's not like you,' she said.

'I know.'

'So you've been looking after him?'

'Yes.'

She leant against the counter, her elbows against her breasts as she sipped from her mug, holding it with both hands. Claude looked at the edge of her nipples, just visible on either side of her arms, which pressed her breasts together.

'That's nice, it shows a caring side to you,' she said.

'He's no financial threat to us, I just have to give him money from time to time.'

'Well it's good you got it,' she said, patting his fly playfully.

He watched her shower before returning to his house. It was almost ready for her to move in and when she did Claude wanted Bertrand out of the way.

7

CLAUDE BOUGHT THE MERC USING TWO CREDIT CARDS. IT was a Polar White E-Class saloon, and knocked him back a cool 33 and a half K. He could picture Maxine in it. As soon as he smelt the leather seats he wanted to fuck her on them. He drove it to Spike's Essex house, gated, security guards, the whole bit. It was Sunday and Maxine was visiting Doris. Spike looked unchanged, muscled, scarred, and deadly. He was six two, and had bright green eyes that twinkled when he spoke, giving him the look of a man about to tell a joke. But when you looked at his face, and the angry scar that ran across his chin, you knew there was little humour coming your way. As Claude looked at him he felt himself sinking into who he used to be.

'So Claude, how's it going?' Spike said with the same lilt, half-mocking, half-friendly in a sinister way, he'd had as a teenager when Claude used to fence his stolen goods.

'Good Spike, good.'

Spike showed him around his house, to which he'd added several wings. He showed him the pool, a woman next to it lying on her stomach reading a magazine. Claude looked down at her naked back.

'This is Kathy,' Spike said. 'I told you Claude was coming round.'

'Pleased to meet you,' she said.

She reached up a hand and Claude caught a glimpse of her breasts. Claude grinned, briefly, stopping himself, in case Spike saw it. Maxine had better tits that Kathy. It was the first time Claude had felt he had something better than Spike. Kathy was a bleached blonde, a good-looking one but she had the used air of a woman who'd been acquired. Looking down at her, and her full buttocks beneath her lime green bikini bottom Claude felt aroused, and it wasn't so much by her as by the fact that he had something better than Spike at home. He thought of how tight Maxine's buttocks were, and of the way they showed a hint of bush when she bent down. Kathy was a looker all right, he had no doubt she was a good shag, she wasn't fat, but there as more of her and he didn't want any more than Maxine. He could feel Spike's eyes on him and he turned to look at him. He got the sense Spike was measuring his attraction to Kathy, as if she was on offer.

Spike showed him the pool room with the deer heads on the wall.

'I shot that fucker,' Spike said.

'Nice, very nice.'

'Shot more than that animal,' Spike said, winking.

Claude felt sixteen again, and remembered how little he'd felt and how Spike's friendship propped him up. He noticed how he was reverting to a working-class idiom and wondered if he was shamming it with Maxine, all those posh places he took her to.

Spike showed him the gardens and the fountain. He showed him the bar.

'You're better stocked than a pub,' Claude said.

'See me old son, I entertain important people here. I had to smarten up a bit to deal with my business associates.'

Claude looked at Spike in his Savile Row suit. He could see the marks of the earrings he used to wear, the faded tattoo on his wrist.

'What do you think of Kathy?' Spike said.

'Tasty.'

'Got rid of the wife. Oh dear, what a slag, but that's another story. I shag Kathy and who I fucking want to me old son, know what it mean?'

'And why not?'

'Why not indeed?'

'Drink?'

'I'll have a whisky.'

Claude told him what he wanted as Spike swigged the Glenfiddich, his eyes like a shark's above the deep golden malt.

'Pleased to hear you found yourself a woman,' Spike said when he'd finished.

'I just want this guy taken out of it, know what I mean?'

'Course I do me old son. And I owe you one, I always said come to me if you need anything.'

'It wasn't that bad inside.'

Spike pointed his finger at him.

'You're not a grass Claude. Not many mates would have done time for me, OK so it was only a short spell, but I ain't forgotten it.'

'Thanks Spike.'

'We grew up together, remember kicking the ball around at the end of the street and that old cow who used to yell at us when I booted it into her garden? Oh fuck me, those were the days, not a care in the world, not a care in the fucking world, except when me old man took his belt to me.'

'You're a mate,' Claude said.

'I always watched out for you.'

Claude gave him the pictures he'd taken of Bertrand and his address. He drove back to Maxine smelling Pina coladas and the wild abandon of the Caribbean.

He made love to her hungrily. Afterwards as they lay there he looked at her and said, 'The house is ready for you'.

I DIDN'T TAKE HER LONG TO ASK ABOUT THE BUSINESS. THEY were eating lunch at Café Rialto in Fulham when she did.

'You never talk about work,' she said, 'you're so unlike other men, that's what I like about you.'

'I don't want to bore you,' Claude said.

'Bore me? How could you bore me?'

'You know men like to show off, I always thought that was off-putting to a woman. And I don't want to put you off.'

Their orders arrived, Maxine had picked the Pollo crema e funghi, Claude the Agnello scottadito. He looked at her there, sitting opposite him, his beautiful dame, her deep brown eyes and her delicious cleavage showing through the top of her indigo blouse and he glanced out of the window beyond her gaze. A van was passing by with the word Blue on it, he couldn't read the rest.

'You want me to talk about Blue Boats?'

'Is that what it's called? Your company?'

Claude nodded.

'It's based on the South Coast, I let my manager take care of things. The money comes in and I spend it on you, now I'd call that a good arrangement.'

'I guess you make most money in the summer,' Maxine said cutting into the chicken.

He watched her chew, her mouth moist, her eyes holding his.

'Yes, but I also lease pleasure cruises, you know the kind of thing business men like. They take on models and party.'

'I know the kind of thing.'

'Then there's the regulars who come out of season and want the sea.'

She didn't ask any more over lunch. Claude tucked into the lamb, it was good, moist, but not as moist at Maxine's mouth as she sucked the chicken and mushrooms from her fork and dropped her napkin. Claude bent down to get it and she parted her toned brown legs beneath the table, showing him she wasn't wearing any underwear. All through the meal he thought of what he wanted to do to her when they got home. She was a constant seduction, just there at arm's reach. He wanted her more and more each time, and he knew he was hooked. Sometimes he thought she was putting on a show for him and he didn't care.

Late that night as she slept he went down to the room he used as an office. He bought a company online and named it Blue Boats. Then he ordered some stationary and got it sent express. He drank a whisky and tried to think of other questions she might ask. Then he went upstairs and got into bed next to Maxine and touched her as she slept. She stirred briefly as his hand wandered between her thighs. He kept touching her, arousing himself, feeding on the knowledge that she was his. She didn't seem to mind anything that he did to her in bed.

9

THE NEXT MORNING CLAUDE WOKE UP AND WONDERED how much it would cost to buy a boat, maybe just a small one. If she asked to visit Blue Boats he'd need an excuse ready. He looked online while she showered, angry he was missing out on his usual morning routine of sitting on the tub watching her lather her breasts.

They were all too much. The cheapest Claude could find, a boat that was way too small but just might convince Maxine he owned the company, came in at 25 K used. And he didn't have it. He was running out of dough. The money he'd kept from the job he did for Spike was almost gone. He'd used it on the holiday and the renovation and on Maxine and he began to feel a small twinge he knew too well. It was what Claude called wallet ache. He'd use his credit cards until he figured out how to get more. And in the meantime, he'd keep her in London. Better that way, away from any discoveries about him. Maybe held do another job for Spike and buy a boat. He could picture Maxine on deck, naked, oiled up, sipping a colada.

When he went upstairs she was doing exercises in the bedroom in a pair of peach pink panties, no bra. Claude lingered in the doorway watching her tits bounce. It was like an ad right there in his bedroom. An ad that said sex is on its way. He thought about where he'd take her to eat and Bertrand's face flickered into his mind.

He distracted himself with her body, with every inch of it. Maxine saw him watching her and she started jogging on the spot.

'I thought I'd take you shopping,' Claude said.

'Do you like these panties?' Maxine said.

'Oh yeah. They fit you really well.'

'They're not too young for me?'

'Young? Are you crazy?'

'I like the colour.'

'So do I Maxine,' Claude said, looking at the outline of her pussy against the skintight material. 'I like everything you wear.'

Over breakfast she handed him the card she found in his jacket.

'It's OK, I know how lonely guys get sometimes,' she said.

He looked down at it, briefly disconnected from the name Exotic Escorts. He felt himself flush.

'It's not what it looks like,' he said, searching for an explanation.

'I don't object to it.'

'I didn't use them. I thought about it, curiosity, you know.'

'Claude you don't need them now you've got me, right?'

'I didn't even remember I had it.'

'I found it in that jacket you wanted me to launder. I wasn't snooping, no big deal, right?'

'Right.'

As she got ready to go out he found the credit card statements detailing his use of escorts with a number of companies. Most of them had been classy hookers, but cheap. He shredded them and emptied the paper into the kitchen bin. Then he tied the refuse bag up and took it outside to the large dustbin.

All through the day Claude thought of Bertrand. He thought of him as he watched Maxine try on skirts and blouses in the changing rooms of department stores, he thought of him as he took her to lunch. And he saw his hands touch her body. And he wondered how much pleasure he gave her in bed, this good-looking intruder who didn't belong in what Claude had planned for him and Maxine.

10

SPIKE HIRED DREDGER, AS HE WAS KNOWN IN THE BUSINESS. Dredger used to be a diver and knew ways of disposing of bodies so they wouldn't be found until they were too badly decomposed to be of any use to forensics. He was a six foot wall of muscle with blazing eyes that hovered between psychosis and an innate hatred for his fellow man. The only time the schizoid light in them abated was when he was handed enough cash to satisfy his crack habit. Then he would retire to his grimy flat and remain in a steady fix that removed the outside world from his knowledge. Dredger liked to stay at home and read about Roman coins, and handle his collection, feeling the history between his dirty tobacco-stained thumbs. Most of the time he didn't look at you. He was lost in a past that consisted of a childhood full of violence and a need to commit bodily harm.

The morning he followed Bertrand he watched him leave his house, walk to the Tesco round the corner and come out some fifteen minutes later with two grocery bags. He returned to his house, where his wife Sandra pecked him on the cheek as he handed her the shopping in the kitchen.

'I think that's everything,' he said.

She peered inside the bag.

'That's it.'

She was a pretty woman with a full figure. As she bent to place the items in the fridge, Bertrand looked at the curve of her arse inside the tight mauve skirt she was wearing, and he thought of Maxine. He'd noticed she'd moved and was thinking of contacting her again. As he looked at Sandra, and her full bust, he thought about the things Maxine did for him in bed. Sandra was pretty bordering on beautiful, with soft green eyes and a sensuous mouth that Bertrand loved to kiss. But she was clean and he needed something extra for his pleasures. He always enjoyed making love to her as she moved beneath him, panting, the rhythm of her breath increasing until she closed her eyes in orgasm, but for a man like Bertrand that was not enough. He thought of undressing her there and taking her on the counter among the clean plates and spices. And he thought of Maxine and how she knew from the first time what turned him on. He could see both women naked, compliant, a mirror to his sexual needs, and he wondered who was lying. He felt aroused and conspicuous, and a small ribbon of shame burned under his collar as his wife bent over the fridge.

'Something wrong?' Sandra said.

'What could be wrong when I have a woman like you?'

'You're such a charmer. But sometimes I wonder.'

'Wonder what?'

'You know, about other women.'

'You think I'm playing around?'

'No. It's just you're the kind of guy who women would make a play for.'

He never answered her in words when she brought this topic up. It wasn't a regular occurrence but she did from time to time. Bertrand always took her to the bedroom. And that is what he did as Dredger loitered under a lamppost thinking of what he was going to do to this posh cunt. As Bertrand peeled Sandra's skirt from her body, undid her blouse and unhooked her bra, Dredger saw knives and hooks. As Bertrand ran his fingers around Sandra's nipples until they stood out from her beautifully proportioned breasts, Dredger wanted to hear Bertrand scream. He thought of all the ways he would make the job Spike had given him enjoyable, losing sight of what he'd been told to do and allowing his need for violence to give him an adrenaline high as he waited in the street, and smelt crack rising from the gutter like a perfume on a woman's neck.

Inside the house Bertrand lowered Sandra's G-string and felt her wetness as she yielded, pulling him onto the bed and guiding him inside her, her eyes open but not for long, her face aroused and secure in the knowledge of him there on top of her as the day passed outside their window. It was Sandra who screamed that morning as Bertrand licked a drop of sweat from her neck and Dredger had his dark thoughts in the street below.

Afterwards Bertrand got dressed and said he was meeting a friend and would be back for dinner. He thought he'd go and try to find Maxine. He never made it past the end of the road. As he turned the corner where an alley ran past the final house the side door on a dirty white van slid open. There was no one around, and the van blocked the view from the house opposite to what occurred on the other side of it. Dredger jumped out in a black balaclava, put a hood over Bertrand's head, and bundled him inside. Bertrand punched out in the darkness as Dredger knocked him out with a right hook. Then he tied his arms and legs with duct tape.

When Bertrand came to he was staring at a concrete ceiling in a boat house.

'OK, no use fighting,' Dredger said, bending over him.

'Who are you?'

'Don't matter who I am.'

'What do you want with me?'

'What do you think I want with you?'

'Is this about money?'

'Bit of a playboy are you?'

'Is this about Maxine? Is that it, is she married?'

Dredger lit a Players and blew smoke towards the ceiling. He leaned against the wall, one foot against the brickwork.

'Tell me about it, shagging all those birds.'

'She's married isn't she? Has her husband sent you?'

'Fancy yourself, don't ya?'

Dredger came away from the wall and placed the burning tip of the cigarette against Bertrand's cheek, gazing into his eyes with animal pleasure. He thought of the things Bertrand saw in female eyes as he aroused them, and aroused himself on the fear he saw in his captive's face. He was going to enjoy this.

Spike had told him about Bertrand, called him a gigolo who was messing around with a mate's bird, and simply said, 'Get rid of this bloke.' Dredger thought he would do it the slow way, then go on a two week high among his coins.

'How much?' Bertrand said.

'How much what?'

'Money, how much do you want?'

'This isn't about money but how much I'm going to hurt you.'

'Why?'

'Orders.'

'What orders?'

'You still shagging her? Maxine?'

'I haven't seen her for ages. This is all a big mistake.'

'She good?'

'I always wondered about her if you must know. I can't believe she's married, I think she's a professional, but not obvious, she never asked for money.'

'You mean she's a hooker?'

'Not in the way you mean.'

'And what other way is there?'

'There are women who operate outside escort services, but are doing it for the money. She behaves like one of them but I never paid her a penny.'

'Then how is she a hooker?'

'She uses sex as casually as a hooker, she's too complaint with what a man wants.'

'But she doesn't want money.'

'The difference between her and a hooker is she picks the men she wants and goes for their income on a big scale, house, bank account.'

'Not a one-off payment for a shag?'

'That's right.'

Dredger was curious now, not expecting him to talk so much, wondering about Maxine.

'What's she like in bed?'

'Extremely good. Don't you see this is all a mistake?'

'Tell me about her.'

'What do you want to know?'

'What does she do?'

'She does whatever you want and she knows what you want. She did things for me the first night that would normally take place weeks later in a relationship.'

'What sort of things?'

'I'm not talking about kinky things. She bypasses the usual foreplay and goes straight to what it is you are turned on by.'

'And what are you turned on by?'

'I need some water.'

Dredger took a final drag on his cigarette, dropped it to the ground and stamped it out. He saw a film, a series of images of naked bodies, prone, engaged in sexual acts, women Bertrand had fucked and he began to replace Bertrand as the actor with himself in the film.

He thought of all the ways this man had enjoyed women, and the few he'd known. Most of those had been low-rent hookers. Those who hadn't been had usually ended up with black eyes and broken arms. For female pleasure was a mystery that threatened Dredger and as he looked down at Bertrand, Dredger hated him, hated what he knew about the opposite sex. He was unaware of his erection as he lifted Bertrand's head and poured some Highland Spring down his throat until he began to choke. Bertrand turned his head sideways, water streaming from his mouth as he gasped for air.

And Dredger saw him glance up at him, and the look of fear as his gaze lingered momentarily on his fly. His jeans were open and it was clear that he was aroused. Dredger turned his back and zipped up. Then he took a length of chain from the wall. It had a hook on the end and he began to wrap it around Bertrand's legs, thinking of all those women.

'Please,' Bertrand said, the tone pitiful, 'I have a wife, don't do this, let me go.'

'You got a picture of her?'

'Who? My wife?'

'Maxine, a picture of Maxine.'

'Yes. In my pocket, let me get it.'

'If I untie you, no funny stuff, and I want you to give me her address.'

'Sure.'

Dredger stood up and looked down at him. He liked these jobs best, the slow easy ones with sexual conversation at their midst. He'd hire some hookers later, maybe two. He thought about what Bertrand had, imagining his upbringing and felt soiled, a piece of litter in the room.

He took a filleting knife from a drawer at the far end of the boat house, gazing out of the cracked window pane at the Thames as it snaked into the distance, the sun setting low over it, the water yellow where it reflected it, like broken egg yolk sinking into mud. Then he walked back to Bertrand and sliced the duct tape from his arms and waited as he fumbled in his pocket. Bertrand made his move, kicking upward at Dredger's groin. But Dredger closed his knees over Bertrand's foot.

'Too slow.'

'Don't you want to see her?' Bertrand said.

Dredger smiled, reached behind him and pulled a Luger from his jeans. Then he blew a hole straight through the middle of Bertrand's head, watching the blood pool on the plastic sheeting he was lying on. He placed the muzzle against Bertrand's ear and blew another one into his face. He always did this to make sure. He'd learned the trick off a hit man in the North of England who sold used cars when he wasn't killing people for money. He used hollow points for maximum internal damage. And Dredger enjoyed the fact that he'd destroyed Bertrand's looks as he fished in his pocket and pulled out his wallet. The only picture it contained was one of a smiling Sandra. He looked at her and put her in his pocket. He cut Bertrand's stomach open to let out any gases, wrapped Bertrand up in the plastic sheeting and opened the door. Then he weighted his body down with chains and dumped him in the river. The place where Dredger had shot Bertrand was a disused boathouse on a stretch of the Thames that saw little traffic. Dredger watched him sink, then returned home, where he called Spike and told him it was done.

11

SPIKE MET CLAUDE A FEW DAYS LATER. HE STOOD THERE IN his suit, chalking his cue as they knocked a few balls around.

'Bertrand won't bother you no more,' Spike said.

'So what did you do?'

'I didn't do nothing me old son. I never seen the geezer.'

'Are you sure he won't bother me again?'

Spike walked right over to him, breathing out the scent of whisky.

'He's at the bottom of the river.'

They went through to the bar and Spike poured them both a Glenfiddich.

Claude thought of Maxine's body, his now.

'Bring her round, your woman. We can all eat,' Spike said.

He slapped Claude on the shoulder, his hand like a lead weight.

Claude enjoyed a few days with Maxine knowing he had no rival. He made love to her every night and watched her shower in the mornings, the soap running off her nipples as he sat on the edge of the tub sipping coffee. Her body looked aroused through the glass shower door, a permanent erotic invitation. And as he sat there Claude wondered what she did for Bertrand. His face sank beneath Claude's consciousness, redundant, irrelevant.

A few days later he drove her to Spike's Essex mansion, watching as she took in the grounds. He searched for interest or desire in her face.

Kathy was wearing a low cut black dress and high heels and Spike a casual suit. Claude watched as he kissed Maxine. She was wearing the dress he'd picked out for her, pink, tight, expensive, tasteful. It didn't show her cleavage, not like Kathy's, she showed too much, almost all the way down to the nipples as she bent to fiddle with her handbag, a tiny thing no bigger than a fist. Claude had decided to put on the casual blue trousers he wore when he took Maxine on their first date in Cuba, they made him feel relaxed. Maxine had picked out the white shirt she liked to peel off him as she stood in only her G-string before they made love. Claude thought he looked right, glancing at himself in the huge mirror in Spike's living room, he didn't have anything to prove. Not with Maxine on his arm. Not with Bertrand out of the way.

Spike's chef, Paulo, cooked for them. He was a dark haired Colombian, well-muscled, Claude figured doubled as a body guard. His eyes lingered on Kathy's tits as he poured her a glass of Sauvignon Blanc. Kathy tapped his thigh as he finished, moving like a waiter in a top restaurant, never spilling a drop. He didn't eye

Maxine, but Claude figured he had something going on with Kathy.

Spike was charming, respectful with Maxine, never once flirted throughout the dinner. They had salmon, then beef served with mixed vegetables. Claude kept thinking Spike had an angle, knowing him, going back so many years. And all through dinner Claude felt he was about to be presented with a bill he couldn't afford to pay.

'Great chef,' Claude said, as they had cognacs in the bar, sitting next to Maxine on a sofa, Spike standing behind Kathy's chair proprietorially.

'He is me old son, and it's a pleasure to have such charming company, ain't it Kath?'

Kathy did a Sharon Stone, crossed her legs slowly, eyes locked on Claude's. It was clear she didn't have any panties on, and he caught a glimpse of shaved between her brown thighs. He thought he detected a move from Spike just before she did it, a squeeze of the shoulder, but he told himself he was mistaken, unless that was a turn on to him, getting his bird to show her peach after dinner. Still, Claude wasn't interested, what Maxine had between her legs was far more tempting, although on her day he fancied that Kathy could give him a good ride. She was fit for her age, which he estimated to be about eight years older than Maxine. As he looked at her he wondered if her tits were real.

They left at around midnight and Spike waved them goodbye all the way out of the estate. Back at his house Claude never felt higher on Maxine's body as he entered her in the bedroom. He searched her face in the half-light and saw only desire and compliance. And he felt bigger than Spike as he spent himself inside her.

12

The money was getting to be a problem. Claude
thought back to the last big amount he'd made, fencing
for Spike, covering for him. And before that when he
used to work. He'd stolen quite a few paintings in his
time, knew the ones that he could flog cheap. He liked
going for the modern artists like Emins, or nudes in
posh areas he felt excluded from as a kid. Walking
around a hallway in Richmond gave him a hard on. He
once caught a glimpse of a housewife sleeping naked
one summer when, high on coke he'd nicked a Klimt.
He stood there looking at her bush as the street lamp
illuminated her body, and wanting to fuck her, thinking
rapists get no free rides in the nick, but an art thief was
another matter. She was expensive tasteful, and nude, a
painting in herself, part of the pleasure of that night,
part of the high.

He handed the painting over to Spike, who flogged it
to an Arab colleague, gave him a small percentage
which he blew on whores. He was good at it, it suited
him back then, with his size. He was good at getting in
and out of windows. But he didn't want to go back
inside so he'd knocked it on the head before Cuba. Now
he began to think of doing one more job, to pay for

Maxine, maybe a big one, something to retire on. He knew of houses where they had Rembrandts, but the problem was without Spike he wouldn't be able to sell it. And if Spike knew he was back in the business he'd start calling in favours.

He wanted to pay for all the things Maxine wanted. He wondered if he spent even more on her what she'd do in bed. Maybe later on she'd need a boob job, he wouldn't want them bigger, they were the right size now, but he wouldn't want to see them sag. Claude began to think of other avenues for selling a painting, and he drew blanks.

The stationary arrived, showing the word Blue Boats in large indigo letters on top grade paper. He left some lying around so Maxine could see them. If she did she didn't say anything. She didn't seem interested in his work at all. She was interested in sex, any time he wanted it.

She began to show Claude things, slowly, subtly allowing him to find his way there in bed. It began with the furry handcuffs she left on the chair in the bedroom. Then it went onto the pantyhose and the time she rode him in stilettos. She shackled him to the bed, teased him, then got dirty with him, and he liked it, liked the feeling of her on top, then being uncuffed and being a little bit rough with her, not hurting her of course, he'd never do that. The first time he did she screamed, then asked him to do it to her again. And he did, all the time wondering how she could be so many women in bed. But he never tired of her, and she never tired of shopping. It was like she was paying him back that way and that felt good. He used to watch her in the changing rooms of expensive stores, naked, touching herself, saying, 'Does this fit me?' as she put something on. And he'd imagine what she'd offer back at the house. She was his now, after all. And Claude had never felt bigger in his life.

Then one day Al turned up. Maxine was upstairs in the shower and Claude stood at the door wondering what he wanted.

13

'WHAT'S UP?' CLAUDE SAID.

'Yvonne's back.'

'Since when? You better come in.'

'I thought you ought to know.'

He took Al into his office and closed the door.

'She came to my gaff with this bloke, big geezer, figured him to be her latest. She's still a looker.'

'What the fuck's she want?'

'Didn't say just told me to pass on her regards.'

'What the fuck's that mean?'

'Dunno.'

'Well if she comes here I ain't talking to her, walking out on me like that.'

'Maybe you should see it from her point of view, she told me Claude.'

'About what?'

'You and them hookers.'

'Did she?'

'She said you used to have a habit, using escort services, that's why she left.'

'There's more to it than that.'

'Well, anyway, it's none of my business.'

'Why'd she go round to your gaff? There something you ain't telling me?'

'No, honest. I think she wanted me to pass on the message.'

'She'll be round, I'm telling ya.'

'Well, what do you want me to do about it?'

'Get rid of her.'

'Na, that ain't my style, I don't do women.'

'I don't mean that, I ain't asking you to beat her up.'

'What then?'

'If she shows again tell her I've moved.'

'I don't think she will.'

'She leave a number?'

'No.'

'Thank for letting me know,' Claude said, standing up.

He showed Al to the door.

'Why did you ask me to tell Maxine I was a van driver?'

'Because I don't want her knowing what a thug you are.'

14

DREDGER HAD SPENT DAYS IN HIS FLAT HIGH ON CRACK, looking at his coins ever since he'd killed Bertrand and watch him sink below the surface of the Thames. He'd fingered the picture of Sandra so much her smile was coated with nicotine. He'd touch her mouth and imagine what she was like. And he wondered about Maxine, the bird at the centre of the hit. The reason for the hit always interested him, he considered it was where the money was. And he wanted a piece of them, these women who lay beyond his reach.

The morning he walked to Sandra's house he was so high on crack he didn't smell the foul odour that rose from his unwashed clothes. He hadn't changed or bathed in days and stubble coated his face. He stood outside the house and looked up at the windows. He thought he'd tell her about her husband, how he played around, maybe she'd give him a shag out of anger.

But more than Sandra he wanted Maxine, he wanted to look at her. He wanted to see what she was like in bed to be worth killing for. He was the one who'd done it, after all. So he deserved a fuck. He realised he needed to change his image, get more money if he was going to get her into bed. Bertrand had said she behaved like a hooker, so she'd do it for money.

He'd spent what Spike had given him for the job, 2K didn't go far these days. And he wanted a lot more than that. He thought about the Russians he'd met a few weeks ago in the pub. And Dredger reckoned they could be his way to Maxine. He had a number for one of them back at his flat, what was his name? Vladimir, that was it.

Now he was big time, bigger than Spike. Dredger figured Sandra wasn't at home, so he walked back to his flat and made the call.

15

Vladimir sat in the London Marriott Hotel bar drinking whisky. He'd always said to Grigory that when he came to England he'd consume a fine malt every day and fuck a new woman every night. He'd read about the English women through copies of The Sun sneaked in to him in Moscow before Communism fell apart and became the place it was now. Vladimir like the new order, him and his buddies with guns. He particularly liked the idea of the English women's readiness to show their tits, although his early experience of them was less than satisfactory. Now he knew which ones to go for, which ones would do it and for how much.

He told them he made his money out of commodities acquisitions, told them how he sold a ton of gas and took the money with him. Theft was not a word that existed in his narrow vocabulary. His mind was engaged in violence and sexual acts that came straight off a porn set. That evening as rain set in over London, he was watching a woman in a cocktail dress lean over a table. He caught a glimpse of nipple, and a flash of something, a piercing he thought. He'd find out later if she had others lower down. He liked to stick his tongue in them.

Grigory followed his line of vision to the edge of her buttocks, just visible beneath her skirt. The woman glanced round and checked them out, what they were wearing. Vladimir fingered the edge of his track suit jacket and then dropped his hand to the heavy gold chain around his wrist. It said smart casual in the bar and this bitch looked away like he wasn't good enough, went and mingled with the guys in suits standing over at the far end of the bar. He could buy any fucking clothes he wanted.

Vladimir was tall, had that military look of toned muscles, not too big like a body builder's, but hard as steel and embedded in his gait. The scar that ran the length of his chin ended in a question mark at his collar. He thought it looked good against a designer shirt. He'd got it in a knife fight as a teenager when he'd taken someone's eye out. He didn't fight any more, he paid others to do that.

Grigory was well-built, with small eyes that weighed everyone up. He wore a permanent look of mistrust and when he smiled it served only to accentuate the appearance of cynicism. He had the physique of a weight lifter and a shaved head. And he had these big hands.

'You said ve meet someone today,' Grigory said.

'Dis guy Dregger, da vun who call, he say he vant do business vith me,' Vladimir said, setting his glass down, looking at his reflection in the polished table top, eyeing two women, one blonde, one brunette, as they came in looking around at who was there.

'Vat business?' Grigory said, following Vladimir's gaze, and watching the brunette, enjoying the swing of her breasts inside her loose blouse.

'He say he is killer, maybe ve can use him then screw him.'

'Screw him?'

'Get rid of him. Vat you tink I am, gay?'

'You vant fuck dem?' Grigory said, nodding in the direction of the women.

Vladimir went up to the bar and ordered more whisky. Grigory watched him talk to the brunette, then enter her number in his i Phone. A vague sense of hostility wrestled with his dependence on his boss. Without Vladimir he'd still be doing time in prison for the murder of that prick who stole his motorbike.

They were ordering bar snacks, tiny cuts of salmon and an assortment of olives, when Dredger turned up. He'd bought a new shirt and looked out of place in the bar full of wealthy businessmen and women looking to pull. He saw Vladimir sitting by the bar, recognised him from the pub when he'd got talking to him about business, and wandered over.

'Sit down,' Vladimir said, putting Dredger's hand in a squeeze that left it numb. 'Dis is Grigory.'

Grigory shook and watched as Vladimir talked to Dredger.

'Drink?' Vladimir said.

'I'll have what you're having.'

Vladimir snapped his fingers at the barman who was standing at the next table clearing glasses.

'Glenfiddich,' he said.

'So vy you contact us?' Grigory said.

'I know some of Vladimir's connections.'

Vladimir nodded.

'Dat's right.'

'I did a job for one of them a while back.' Dredger sipped his whisky, sizing Grigory up, seeing him as a competitor, he could see it in his eyes, he could smell the territoriality. 'I can do a job for you if you're looking.'

'Ve alvays looking but how good are you?' Vladimir said.

'They never find the bodies when I do the work.'

Vladimir nodded, then leaned forward.

'Vat are your methods?'

'Any fucking thing I can get my hands on.'

'I like, I like,' Vladimir said, laughing.

'I favour a knife or a gun.'

All the while Grigory didn't take his eyes off Dredger. He turned his tumbler round and round on the polished table.

'How much you charge?' Grigory said.

Dredger looked at Vladimir as he answered.

'It depends.'

'On vat?' Vladimir said.

'The job.'

'I need to know how expensive you are.'

'I range from 2 to 25.'

Vladimir blew air at him.

'2 is normal but 25, you must be killing the fucking President for that.'

'Like I say, it depends on the job.'

'If I hire you, you better be good.'

'I am.'

'Or I send Grigory after you.'

'You got my number.'

'OK ve be in touch,' Vladimir said. 'If I vant you I call you.'

Dredger emptied his glass. He shook hands with them, squeezing Vladimir's tight, Grigory's tighter, and left the bar.

'You tink he any good?' Grigory said as he watched him walk away.

'I hear he has carried out jobs. Maybe ve use him to get rid of that arsehole Harry Simmons.'

'Vot if he fuck it up?'

'Den ve shoot him.

'You gonna pay him?'

'Maybe first time, in de end ve use him and get rid of him. I don't vant vun of our guys tangling vit Simmons.'

16

WHEN BERTRAND WENT MISSING SANDRA CALLED THE police. Despite his affairs he was always punctual in his habits with her. The two police officers who spoke to her put in the usual report that did nothing to assure her they were looking for her husband. Days passed, days in which she drank, unusual for her. Days in which she called friends, and searched his pockets for clues, driving to places she knew he went to meet friends for drinks. Bertrand's photography business didn't help. She couldn't access his client list, and a brief scan of his computer showed only portrait shots, not the nudes Bertrand took of the women he seduced. He'd hidden those, together with his frequent affairs, which arose from casual encounters in bars and jobs he'd take on from the bored and affluent wives of wealthy businessmen. Bertrand's life had been one of sexual pleasure-seeking and disguise. And in her hunt for her husband Sandra found herself unable to advance beyond a basic sense of what his movements were. They were much as she expected them to be, and the fact that she discovered nothing out of the ordinary added to her concern.

When his body was discovered floating in the river the police identified him. Dredger had failed to seal the plastic wrapping and the weights had become dislodged. Although he was badly decomposed a week later, Dredger had failed to search his pockets thoroughly. Bertrand was in the habit of carrying two wallets, his married one, containing the credit cards his wife knew about and whose statements she often checked for him, and his seducer's one, containing two cards she didn't know about. He'd registered these to the small studio he rented a few blocks away from where he lived. It was from these credit cards that the police identified him.

They turned up on her doorstep one morning when she'd been unable to sleep and push away the notion that something had happened to Bertrand. The two officers were polite and respectful in a bureaucratic manner. They drove her through the distant streets to identify the body and she heard someone howl in the sterile room. Then they drove her home and left her with a hole in her heart she lived inside in the ensuing days of alcohol and sleeplessness.

Sandra felt herself becoming unreal as she wandered the empty home trying to understand what had happened. Friends visited and she sat there looking at their faces, thinking of Bertrand. When they left she'd stagger to Tesco and buy more wine and drink alone, clutching a photograph of her and Bertrand on holiday the year before.

Sandra asked herself who would want her husband dead. Her mornings were spent drinking coffee, calling friends and inquiring if they knew anything that could shed light on what had happened. Her inquiries were met with the dismissal of the idea that anyone would want to harm Bertrand, but a few awkward silences prompted her to dig more deeply into what there was about her husband's life she didn't know.

Finally one friend told her, and Sandra put down the phone and stared at the portrait of her and Bertrand that sat in the living room, and wondered how long he'd been unfaithful to her and with whom. Her friend hadn't told her much, only that she'd heard he'd seen another woman. She'd added it was some time ago and probably a one-off. The double discovery of his murder and separate life made her obsessive and watchful. She began to go through the address book in his phone.

One name that stood out was Maxine's. There were a few women's names she didn't recognise, but Bertrand had entered an address for Maxine.

Sandra went round to Maxine's flat only to be told she'd moved. The new tenant gave her the forwarding address.

One hot day at the beginning of summer, she went to Claude's house and waited in her Audi watching for signs of Maxine, her anger fighting her grief. Finally she saw her. Maxine was returning arm in arm with Claude, and she watched her walk up the path to the front door and go inside.

17

SPIKE INVITED CLAUDE AND MAXINE OVER AGAIN THAT Saturday. Claude could tell Maxine liked the house, she relaxed a bit, let her eyes wander, talked to Spike a little more than she had the time before. Small changes that didn't go unnoticed by Claude. He caught Spike looking at her a few times, his gaze lingering too long. After lunch Maxine was at the bar pouring herself a drink when Claude saw Spike walk up behind here, lay a hand on her arse and hold it there. He waited for Maxine's response but she didn't do anything, just swigged from her glass as Spike walked back. Claude's knuckles were white on his glass as he laid it down, glanced at Spike and went and got another drink.

'So Maxine,' Spike said, 'how did you and Claude meet?'

'In Cuba, I was holidaying with a friend.'

'Me and Kathy are going there ain't we?'

'Yeah,' Kathy said, swigging her cocktail.

She was drunk and Claude watched them all talk.

He went and sat next to Maxine and put his hand on her leg, looking at Spike. He looked at Spike's possessions and thought of Maxine's body beneath her dress. He thought of Kathy, of the flash of pussy he'd seen last time and wondered if this was what Spike wanted, a trade of women, wondered if Kathy did it all the time, maybe it accounted for her drinking habit. He wondered how far Spike would let Kathy go.

Spike didn't make another move on Maxine, but Claude had seen it. He knew Spike's need for acquisition and show. He thought about doing another job, a painting expensive enough to get him want he wanted. The problem was, Spike was still the only bloke he knew with the right connections. And he didn't want to use him. He kept expecting Spike to take him to one side and mention the hit, ask for a taste of Maxine in return, but he didn't. He left early with Maxine. All the way home he thought of Spike's hand on her arse and wondered. He watched her undress in the bedroom later. Then he touched her hungrily, hearing the hiss of the Caribbean Sea as he parted her thighs and entered her.

He was woken by the sound of his own voice in the small hours.

'Don't you ever let me smell another man on you,' he said, his mouth bone dry.

Maxine stirred next to him.

'What?'

He turned over and pretended to be asleep, but when she nodded off again he pulled the sheets down and studied every inch of her naked body. He held her buttocks in his hands and closed his eyes, he ran his fingers between her legs, he tasted her and listened to her breathing, studying her for secret pleasures. He thought of Spike's hand on her and he wondered if she enjoyed it, being touched by another man. And he thought of money, enough money not to need Spike any more.

18

THAT FRIDAY NIGHT VLADIMIR WAS IN THE MARRIOTT WITH a hooker. He was watching her walk naked around the room when the phone went.

'Hello?'

'It's Grigory.'

'Yes Grigory.'

'Our business colleague is becoming a real pain in da arse.'

'Den ve get Dredger to do de job.'

'De sooner de better.'

Vladimir hung up and watched as the hooker bent to put her G-string on. He came up behind her and pulled her by the hand to the bed.

'Vun more,' he said.

Afterwards he paid her, drank a glass of whisky and showered. Then he went down to his Bentley and drove to his offices, deep in Piccadilly.

He sat at his desk and looked at the figures Grigory had emailed him. Harry Simmons had his hand in gun running and other businesses and had been trading with Vladimir. From what Grigory had found out, he'd been short changing him. There was only one thing Vladimir enjoyed more than a hooker, and that was a good profit, and anyone ripping him off was found dead within days.

That evening he phoned Dredger on his mobile.

'Dredger it's Vladimir, I got a job for you.'

#

Dredger met him at a warehouse on the edge of an industrial estate near Hammersmith that Vladimir used for transporting goods.

'So dis de guy I vant you to take out,' Vladimir said, handing Dredger a picture of Harry Simmons.

'How much?'

'Two K. You do dis vun good, I give you bigger job.'

Vladimir gave him the addresses he had for Simmons and half the cash, then walked outside. He locked up his warehouse as Dredger drove away in his white van.

19

Harry Simmons was a large man with a bald head, who wore suits that covered his jailhouse tattoos. He'd been a violent man when younger, did a few bank jobs with a gang called the Crewe boys, so named because of the railway town most of them came from. He'd ended up in Brixton, and spent a few years inside. On the outside he set up a lucrative business selling hardware, franchised that and moved into the gun running business when he met Tony Yallow one day at the dogs, a boxer who'd done time, and shared a cell with him. Yallow won some featherweight titles in South London before getting into the arms business. Yallow had contacts in Dubai and South America, he mixed with the Colombian cartels, made a fortune when they picked London as their money laundering capital after Clinton clamped down on them. The day Harry ran into Yallow he'd lost a K the greyhounds and Yallow took him to dinner, made the proposal and they became partners. Yallow said he was looking for someone he could trust who knew how to handle himself. And Harry did. He was good with his fists but liked using a chainsaw if things got particularly nasty with a customer. He didn't like the Russians, hated

Communists and always ripped them off. He didn't see Dredger coming that Saturday morning.

He'd risen early, called his mistress Diamond, and arranged to go over for quick shag before taking his wife Hilary to the pictures. They used to watch the new releases in Leicester Square before going to a show in Soho, something risky, not too nude, Hilary didn't like seeing pussy, didn't mind a pair of tits swinging at her as she ate. Harry considered Paul Raymond a class act a real businessman, and he always wished he'd met him.

'So much to talk about,' he said.

The sun was out as he left his gated house in Essex, walked down the path to his Jag, smelt his roses, and drove to few miles to the house he'd bought for Diamond. Her real name was Daphne, but she used to dance as Diamond, using snakes and wearing a real diamond in her navel. That was after she got too old for it, although she sometimes did it for Harry. He liked that about her, her sense of fun, Hilary had got too serious, all about money, used to let him shag her but she'd just roll over afterwards. Diamond sometimes went to his office in an overcoat and shades. She'd take them off, nothing underneath, and lie down on the mini golf course Harry had there, as he putted balls between her legs.

Dredger saw him drive to Diamond's, park and get out. Diamond greeted Harry in a pink negligee that he soon removed as she fumbled with his zip.

'Come on let's have a quick one,' Harry said.

'I can't.

'What do you mean you can't? Why do you think I came round here on a Saturday?'

'It's me period, Harry. But, I can always do this for ya.'

Harry held her head as she leant and took him in her mouth, looking out at the verdant lawns he paid for. Afterwards he watched her slip the negligee on and then left.

As he was getting in his car he noticed a semen stain on his trousers. He got a tissue out of his pocket and dabbed at it as Dredger grabbed him from behind, throwing a hood over his head and hauling him into his van that was parked a few metres away. Harry kicked out and swung a punch but Dredger smashed him in the face with a pair of dusters, knocking him out cold. Then he drove him to a garage he used in the East End. It was at the back of a disused industrial area. He drove the van inside, shut the door and put the light on. Then he pulled Harry out. Harry was regaining consciousness when he looked up at Dredger standing over him with a Beretta. Dredger had asked a few questions about Harry, heard about his reputation, and had decided he'd make this one quick. He shot him in the head. Then he burned the body in an incinerator at the back.

20

VLADIMIR WAS IN HIS OFFICE WHEN DREDGER CALLED HIM.

'Simmons won't pose a problem to ya no more,' Dredger said.

'Good, dat vas fast. I like fast ven it comes to hits.'

'He was worth more than 2 K.'

'You tink? Come and get money from Marriott, and we discuss bigger job.'

He hung up and met Dredger that evening at the bar, Grigory watching Dredger without saying anything, juts two hit men with greed and competition killing the dialogue.

'Here is da cash,' Vladimir said, handing him an envelope.

Dredger didn't bother counting it, just slipped it in his inside pocket.

'So you mentioned something bigger.'

'How big you vant to go?'

'You think I can't handle it?'

'Did I say dat?'

'What then?'

'Some jobs need more caution. Tell me, how did you do it to Simmons?'

'I followed him, grabbed him, took him to a place I use and shot him in the head.'

'Vat about da body?'

'I burned it in an incinerator.'

'Good, I like dat. No more Simmons arsehole,' Vladimir said, wiping his hands on a napkin and picking a strand of chicken from his teeth.

'You got anyone else you want taken out?'

'Ya I do, but I must talk to business partner first.'

'Who's that?'

Vladimir nodded at Grigory. Dredger tuned to him and Grigory winked.

Dredger took the money and spent it on some flash new clothes he thought would impress Spike. He'd decided to use the Russians to get enough cash to get into business with Spike, afford all the women he'd always wondered about. He went round there the following evening having called Spike saying he had a business proposition for him.

'Oh dear oh dear where did you get that clobber?' Spike said when he opened the door.

'It's quality stuff.'

Spike felt his lapel, running his eyes down the cheaply tailored suit and grinning.

'You want quality, Dredger, think of the cut on my Savile Row.'

Dredger followed him inside, wondering why Spike was wearing a pair of jeans and a T-shirt. He had mud on his hands and was sweating. He was annoyed with Spike, wanting to impress him.

'What you been up to?' Spike said.

'I met this Russian geezer, he's the big time.'

'Oh yeah?'

'I can introduce you if you want Spike.'

'You think he wants to do business with me?'

'Might do.'

'Come outside and give me a hand before Kathy gets back.'

Dredger followed Spike to the pool and out to the end of the garden. Beneath some trees there was a six foot hole and a large black sack next to it.

'What you up to?' Dredger said.

'Burying my chef Paulo, fucking Colombians.'

'He was a good cook.'

'I know he was a good cook, he was also fucking Kathy, caught them at it earlier. She's gone shopping, something she always does after a shag, as if she's dissatisfied in some way, now help me put him inside and then come and have a drink.'

'You should have called me,' Dredger said.

'Yeah well this one was personal.'

'What did you do?'

'Took him to the end of the garden for a chat and chopped him up with his meat cleaver.'

'She know?'

'No she don't know, she don't know I saw them either, and that's the way it's gonna stay.'

Dredger looked at the blood-spattered tree next to the sack, then he helped him lift the sack in and cover it up with earth.

'You'll need to hose that down,' Dredger said, nodding at the tree.

'I think it's going to rain,' Spike said, looking at the sky, 'besides, who's going to miss him?'

'Kathy is.'

'Well fucking let her.'

CLAUDE BOUGHT MAXINE A NEW DRESS, STRAIGHT OFF THE designer shelves. She looked good in Armani and he liked to watch her bend in a bar, enough cleavage showing but not too much. He liked watching her get dressed, her tight arse bending over her panties as she pulled them on. He enjoyed it both ways, having her and watching other men desire her. It was the place he used to occupy before she came along, the isolation of visual sex temporarily alleviating personal smallness. Once a watcher he was now a player. He noticed how he changed his language with her, dropping it around Al and Spike. He seemed to exist next to the old Claude, the one he'd left in London on a rainy day when he discovered the Caribbean sun.

Maxine would wander around the house with no bra on, make coffee like that, exercise as Claude watched. He asked her if she'd dress up for him, she did. He got her a little maid's outfit and she did the housework in it, dusting the furniture and bending to show him the perfect gap between her legs. And it made him wonder how many men she'd do these things for. He'd take her out to eat and want her all through the meal. When they got home at night he'd unwrap her like a gift. Then he'd see Spike's face.

One afternoon when Claude went to visit Al while Maxine went shopping. She took a taxi and Claude thought it was only a matter of time before he needed to buy her a car. Sandra was waiting outside her house when she returned. She had black lines around her eyes and stood there staring at Maxine, saying nothing for a few moments in which Maxine tried to guess who she was. She thought maybe she was Claude's ex, he'd mentioned Yvonne to her but hadn't talked much about her.

'You knew Bertrand,' Sandra said.

'Who are you?'

'His wife.'

Maxine opened the door, put her bags inside and closed it.

'Not here.'

She walked Sandra down the road.

'You had an affair with my husband,' Sandra said.

'What makes you think that?'

'Things I've been told about him, things I didn't now, that I've only just recently found out. I haven't come here to make a scene, but be straight with me'

'I didn't know he was married.'

'How long?'

'I haven't seen him for months. You said "knew" Bertrand.'

'He's dead.'

Maxine narrowed her eyes.

'Somebody killed him,' Sandra said.

'Who would do that?'

'That's what I'm trying to find out.'

They waked to the local pub, The Fox, and Maxine bought Sandra a few glasses of wine, joining her but nursing the single glass she bought just to settle her nerves over the encounter. She assessed Sandra's state of mind, and whether she was likely to tell Claude if she knew about him. Sandra didn't mention him or having seen her walk arm in arm with a man, instead she began to cry as she said she'd found out her husband was dead and had been cheating on her. Maxine felt sorry for her.

'Everything I thought I knew has been a lie,' Sandra said, dabbing her eyes with a stained tissue, sipping her Pinot Grigio, 'I loved him, I still do, I don't want to believe it.'

'It didn't last long between us. A few weeks, that was all, if I'd known he was married I'd never have done it,' Maxine said.

'I don't think you were the only one.'

'What makes you think that?'

'Things people are saying, numbers I've found in his phone.'

'Who do you think would want him dead?'

'That's what I intend to find out.'

Sandra gave Maxine a different look then, determined, angry and Maxine felt wary of her. After an hour she made an excuse and left her there.

She went home and showered, then put on a pink G-string, pink skirt, and thin blue blouse, no bra. When Claude got home Maxine wrapped her arms round his neck and said, 'Where are you taking me tonight?'

'Where do you want to go?'

'Somewhere new. Then afterwards I want to do something new with you.'

He took her to Claude's Kitchen, thinking how he'd like to own a place like that, name it after himself, maybe even name one Maxine's, he could see it, pink inside, inviting, sexy. Then he thought of the money he owed and the rising debt he was in and the Rembrandt he knew was hanging on a wall in an address not far from there and who he could sell it to. Maxine was the best looking woman in there and Claude felt rich, wanting her there, right there among the other diners. He imagined getting on the table and her straddling him in her heels, raising her skirt and sliding her peach down over his cock as the diners watched them at it.

Maxine ordered an onglet steak and Claude scallops but they shared, dipping forks into each other's plates and gazing across the table. They drank a bottle of Burgundy and returned to the house where she stripped for him, putting the lights down low in the bedroom and removing her blouse slowly, then pressing her tits into his face as she undid his fly. She leant down and took him in her mouth then they did it in the shower, and Maxine seemed someone else again, someone Claude knew but was still discovering and he liked it, this woman who could do it all. She took him into the bedroom and rode him, and her arousal made her face seem even more beautiful than he'd known it to be.

Afterwards as she slept he wandered the darkened house. He wondered about it, her sexual versatility, as if she was inhabited by different women, all of them a turn on, all of them keeping his hunger alive.

22

It wasn't long before he got the next call. It came a week later. Spike's voice was friendly, saying come round for some food, maybe have a swim, nice in this hot weather. Claude didn't mention that part to Maxine, he didn't want her showing too much. But they went there the following Friday evening as the sun set in a deep blue sky. Claude told Maxine to wear one of the new dresses, nothing revealing.

Kathy let them in. She had a low cut blackberry coloured dress on, and kissed Claude on the cheek then Maxine. She showed them into the bar. Vladimir and Grigory were there, so was Dredger. Spike was handing out drinks.

'Claude, Maxine, meet Vladimir and Grigory,' he said.

Vladimir got up and shook their hands, formal, polite in his business suit.

'Pleased to meet you,' he said.

'These are my new business associates,' Dredger said, rising, walking ahead of Spike, 'I'm Dredger.'

Kathy bent to pick her drink up from a table and Claude watched Vladimir as he ran his eyes over her cleavage. Spike got Claude a glass of Sauvignon Blanc, Maxine a Pinot Grigio.

'So Vladimir what line of business are you in?' Spike said.

'Oh I do all deals dat make me money.'

'Covers quite a lot of areas, don't it?'

'Ya, quite a lot.'

'Grigory you work with him?'

'Ya, I help him out.'

'With what?'

'Vatever he needs.'

'That right?'

Spike knocked his whisky back, looking at Dredger. He'd done it deliberately, inviting them round with people they couldn't talk business in front of. He didn't like the fact that Dredger had suggested it, like he was trying to go one up on him. He didn't like Russians, their accents or their clothes.

Claude stayed close to Maxine throughout the evening, getting the measure of these guys, sensing the rising tension. Spike wanted to show them he was in charge but during the course of the evening Vladimir outdid him in boasts and Grigory sat watching the competition between the two men. Kathy got drunk, showed too much thigh, and Claude felt relieved Maxine was wearing the dress he'd picked out.

All evening Vladimir and Spike circled one another. They traded stories, and Claude watched them with interest. He saw Spike stepping out of his depth. And he liked it. It wouldn't cost much, he thought.

23

IT WAS TOWARDS THE END OF THE EVENING SPIKE SUGGESTED they all go for a swim. Vladimir and Grigory slipped out of their trousers and jumped in the pool in their jockeys. Spike pulled his off to reveal a thong. Dredger swam in his Y-fronts. And Kathy pulled off her dress and jumped in the water in her G-string, as Vladimir eyed her tits. They were a good pair, but not as good as Maxine's. Claude wanted to keep her away from it, but she got a bikini from the changing room, a tasteful blue one, put it on in there and got in the pool. Claude found a pair of trunks and joined them for a while, then made an excuse and went back in the changing room with Maxine. He locked the door and they towelled themselves down and got dressed. Then they left, waving at the others in the pool.

As he drove back Spike called up some hookers for Vladimir and Grigory. Dredger watched them as they had sex on the loungers. Spike hadn't ordered one for him. The evening hadn't gone the way he'd planned it and he didn't like it. Later as they left he spoke to Vladimir on Spike's drive.

'Got any more work for me?' Dredger said.

'I'll give you a call.'

Back in Fulham Claude thought about Spike resentfully. He didn't want to go there any more, he wanted to steal the Rembrandt and get enough.

He thought about Vladimir. He'd got his number after dinner and now as Maxine slept he looked at it, thinking about it. If he took the painting he could use the money to stop what he saw was coming. He wasn't going to let Spike get his hands on Maxine. He'd seen the way he looked at her. He'd seen him glance up from the blue surface of the pool as she got out of the water and her bikini showed a bit too much, clinging to her wet body. He thought of the day he saw her getting out of the Caribbean Sea and he wanted Spike out of the way.

The next morning he got up early and as he opened the door to put out the rubbish he found Yvonne standing on his doorstep.

24

SHE HAD HER HAND OUT AND WAS ABOUT TO RING THE BELL.
She looked the same, good-looking but a bit cheap,
peroxided hair, bronze skin, bust popping out of her
blouse, but Claude noticed she was expensively
dressed. He looked over her shoulder for the guy Al had
mentioned but saw only the empty street. He glanced at
his watch.

'Aren't you gonna invite me in?' Yvonne said.

'Bit early ain't it?'

'It's eight. Besides, I know you're an early riser.'

'What do you want?'

'I got a business proposition for you.'

'You got a bloody nerve coming here walking out on
me like that.'

'You know why I did, Claude.'

'Yeah well, you ain't coming back.'

'I don't want to come back, I got a new fella.'

'Yeah, I heard.'

'That brother of yours tell you?'

'What do you think?'

'Is Al still working?'

'No. What is this proposition?'

'My new fella he works in the art business.'

25

HE SLIPPED ON A COAT AND TALKED TO HER IN THE MERC, liking the way Yvonne took in the upholstery. She didn't ask her where he got the money from, just told him what she had in mind.

'Micky's always worked in the business, he used to be an auctioneer,' she said.

'You want me to nick a painting,' Claude said.

'We tried using someone. He wasn't any good.'

'And what makes you think I want to go back to that?'

'The money.'

'Your fella know what he's doing?'

'He's a pro Claude. He's got good contacts.'

'What do you want me to nick?'

'A painting by Cecily Brown.'

'She's modern.'

'I know she's bloody modern and she's good. You like that crowd, remember?'

'She won't bring in much.'

'She sells. This one will.'

'What's the painting?'

'Sweetie.'

'What's it look like?'

'It a beautiful oil of a nice nude lady with a large hard cock inside her, her face says it all,' Yvonne said, reaching into her handbag and handing him a photo.

Claude looked at it, liking it, this painting of a naked woman, classy, sitting on a guy's lap, as he gave it to her, sucking on her nipples. He thought Yvonne was right, nice pinks, good body, erotic, his style. He liked to look at the paintings he stole before he parted with them.

'How much she sell for?'

'This one would get a million.'

'Where is the painting?'

'Private house, I got the keys.'

'How come?'

'I know the owner.'

'Where is it?'

'Richmond.'

'What's my cut?'

'Twenty five percent.'

'I want more.'

'You always want more Claude but you ain't gonna get it.'

26

DREDGER GOT THE CALL TO DO A SECOND JOB FOR VLADIMIR.

'I vant dis guy taken out fast,' Vladimir said, handing him a picture of a fat man in a bar.

They were sitting in his hotel bedroom. Dredger could hear the shower running and saw steam coming out from under the door and he looked at Vladimir, this wealthy Russian he disliked and craved the things he'd acquired. Vladimir passed Dredger details of the target's address and places he frequented. Grigory watched Dredger closely, sitting at the opposite end of the room, his leg slung over his knee.

'Who is he?' Dredger said.

'Manuel Ringer,' Vladimir said.

'What's he done, ripped you off?'

Vladimir looked at him.

'Doesn't matter vat he's done, vat matter is I pay you to kill him.'

There was a moment when Dredger held Vladimir's stare, then he dropped his eyes and tapped the picture.

'How much?' he said.

'2 K straight hit.'

Dredger stood up.

'OK I've had enough of this, I want a big hit, not some minor job. Call me when you have something.'

He threw the picture on the table as a naked woman stepped out of the bathroom. She made no attempt to hide her body and for a moment Dredger was stopped in his tracks. He stared at her huge tits, her waxed pussy and her face. Definitely a hooker, but a classy one, the kind he couldn't afford, not at the moment, but he wanted her. He wanted Maxine most of all, but he'd start with Sandra the wife of that stuck up twat. She'd be nice, she probably had a great pair of tits. But Maxine was another matter. Dredger had got hard in the pool as he watched her in her bikini. She had the body of a model. Not like Kathy, he'd shag Kathy but she was a slut.

Vladimir look at Dredger, noting his interest in the hooker as she dressed, impervious to their gazes. He laid his hand on his shoulder.

'Vat till Candy leaves den ve talk business.'

'All right.'

He watched her sling on her few clothes and leave.

'OK, I vant before and after shots,' Vladimir said. 'You hurt him, take shots then kill him and I pay you good money.'

'How much?'

'10 K and I throw in Candy.'

'That's more like it,' Dredger said. 'But I need to know more about him.'

'OK, vat you vant to know?'

'Who is he, what's he done to piss you off?'

'He businessman who has taken money from me.'

'And you'll throw in the whore?'

'For a full hour.'

Vladimir could tell Dredger expected more, wanted to make a gain on each hit. He walked over to the bar and poured himself a cognac as Dredger stood up and said, 'I'll be in touch.'

'I know you vill,' Vladimir said.

#

Later that day Vladimir met Spike. Spike had told him he had some business interests in areas Vladimir might want to invest in. They met at Spike's house. Spike showed him a file with all the figures.

'OK so ve talk veapons parts, and dis is reputable business. So how much you vant I put in?' Vladimir said, leaning back, looking at Spike.

'The more the better,' Spike said.

Grigory watched the two men measuring one another up.

'I need more information,' Vladimir said.

'Like what?'

'I need more product information.'

'I can get that for you,' Spike said.

'Den ve do business.'

'I hear you're involved in some weapons deals.'

'You want piece of da action?'

'I know people who'd buy,' Spike said.

'Ve are not talking about cheap guns here,' Vladimir said.

'I didn't think so.'

'But vit dis ve could make a lot,' Vladimr said, tapping the file, finishing his whisky, standing up to go.

Grigory watched it all, looking for that moment of submission from Spike. It didn't come and he began to get an idea and it involved a lot of money.

27

Claude found Maxine wanted to please him more and more. Ever since the visit from Sandra she'd felt uneasy, nervous she'd turn up while he was there. She wore the lingerie he liked best, half cut bras, sheer panties, and put on a show while she washed. Every night she gave him what he wanted in bed, new things as well, never pushing the boundary too far, knowing what he liked, knowing it all.

He fed on her body. Eating out he'd count the times men looked at her. He liked them to linger on her body long enough and for her to show no response. It was her response that concerned him, or the lack of it that time Spike laid his hand on her arse.

So long as he smelled the Caribbean on her skin at night everything was all right. Questioning how much Maxine desired him was not something Claude did, instead he focused on holding her where he wanted her, in bed, his, at a table, untouched by others, touched by him alone.

Over breakfast Maxine said, 'I still haven't seen your business, Blue Boats.'

'I'm thinking of selling it,' Claude said.

'You're never short of money and you don't seem to do much work. You must be good.'

'That's the way to do it, especially if you've got a class bird.'

His evasion breathed the air of hers. Together they inhabited a world of fantasy and mutual need.

He lived in a bright new future, a sharp place of acquisitions he laboured to afford. And he planned out the theft. Yvonne had given him the address of the house that contained Sweetie and Claude had hidden the picture that morning he went back inside the house while Maxine slept. He decided to steal the painting the following Friday. The owners would be out during the afternoon, and it would be a straightforward matter of in and out, hand it over to Yvonne and get paid.

He did a recce one evening, drove round to Richmond, walked past the house wearing a baseball hat, checked out the drive. It was as Yvonne had said, she'd done her homework. She'd always been good at that when they worked together. Before he'd given it up and got into escorts.

28

IT WAS A SUNDAY WHEN DREDGER CARRIED OUT THE HIT ON Ringer. He sat outside his house in his van for hours. He stared at the front door from the opposite side of the road. The house was hidden behind hedges deep in St John's Wood. As he sat there Dredger began to realise he hated the wealthy, hated their mannerisms, but he wanted what they had. The idea of envy was as alien to Dredger as his own sexual needs. The existed inside him like a hidden danger he was unaware of, since he lived with the idea that he was too clever for the law. He'd never done time and he never planned to. He'd do the job and get the money. He'd ask for a rise from Vladimir on the next hit. He wanted to maraud the trappings of wealth he saw around him and soil expensive things with his nicotine stained hands. He wanted to touch the skins of rich men's wives, and corrupt them with his sexual needs. He imagined Sandra naked, alone with him, as trapped as one of his targets. He allowed himself the fantasies that sometimes flickered through his mind when he was torturing a target, and focused these on the women he would soon afford, Sandra, Maxine, their white skins soft beneath his hands, their bodies his to do what he wanted with. The screams he conjured from their open mouths as he sat in his van were those of the men he killed. To Dredger there was no line between pleasure and pain, so long as the pain was inflicted on another person.

His coffee had grown cold beside him. He wanted to take a piss and walked to the side of the house and aimed at a bush just as a car left the drive. He glanced over his shoulder, and saw Ringer behind the wheel of the Rolls Royce. He shook himself off and ran to his van. He followed him for miles, hanging back a few cars, until he stopped by an office. He watched him get out and go inside. He was a large man with awkward mannerisms, and he swung his hands in a simian manner as he walked.

After a few minutes Dredger got out and walked past the office. It was a two storey building next to a parking lot. There was no name on the door. Dredger walked back and went inside. The reception area was empty and he heard someone talking on the phone in one of the rooms.

As he opened the door he could see Ringer standing with his back to him.

'These fucking Russians,' he said, 'they rip everyone off.'

Dredger pulled the door to and waited until he heard him hang up. The he went in slowly. Ringer was looking out of the window as Dredger came up behind him. Ringer saw his reflection and turned as Dredger moved in on him.

'Who the fuck are you? Get out of my office,' Ringer said.

Dredger punched him in the face, knocking him to the floor. He peered down at him, Ringer was out cold. He took a phone out of his pocket and took the first two shots of Ringer. It was a pay as you go phone he'd bought with cash and was unregistered. Then he gagged him with duct tape. He walked to the front door and locked it, returning to the office and closing the door as Ringer opened his eyes in alarm. There were no cameras in the building.

Dredger put on the dusters, lifted him up and sat him in a chair. Then he began to work him over, inflicting steady heavy punches on his face, breaking his jaw and knocking out two teeth. He took more shots, saying nothing, enjoying the fear in Ringer's face. He knew what Vladimir wanted for his money and he gave it to him. He burnt him with a Zippo lighter, he broke his ribs. Then he pulled the Luger from his belt and blew Ringer's head off.

29

Claude had gone to see Al that Monday morning. He had a few things he wanted to talk over with him, business matters. He told him about the visit from Yvonne and the planned robbery. Al sat there staring at his mug of coffee as Claude talked. When he finished Al looked at him and shook his head.

'I thought you'd given it up,' he said.

'I had.'

'It's Maxine isn't it? You need the money for her.'

'It ain't like that.'

'I reckon it is.'

'What are you saying, she's a hooker?

'No I ain't saying that.'

'What then?'

'I don't want to see you go back inside.'

'I ain't gonna, trust me.'

'You got it all sewn up ain't ya?'

'I reckon this one's an easy job.'

'No such thing.'

'Why you telling me?'

'I don't know, weird seeing Yvonne again and I don't trust her fella.'

'Oh no,' Al said standing up and putting his hands out in front of him. 'Don't involve me in this.'

'Just in case I need some muscle.'

'No, Claude.'

'I ain't saying it's a cert, but the geezer might try it on.'

'I've beaten enough blokes up for you.'

'Well let's hope I don't need you.'

#

When Claude got back he saw Maxine talking to a woman. He could see she was flustered and that they were arguing. The woman was waving her arms about and Maxine seemed to be trying to placate her. Claude parked and watched as the conversation continued. Finally he got out and walked up to them. Maxine didn't see him, as she had her back to him.

'I want to find out who killed him,' the woman said.

'I don't know,' Maxine said.

'Someone murdered Bertrand, doesn't that mean something to you?'

'Of course.'

'I don't believe we've met,' Claude said, extending his hand.

Maxine turned. Claude could see the tension in her face.

'My name's Sandra, I'm here about my husband.'

She shook his hand and looked away. Tears were dancing in the corner of her eyes, this casualty of his need for Maxine.

'Your husband?' Claude said.

'He's been killed, Maxine knew him.'

'There must be some mistake. Who was your husband?'

'Bertrand,' Maxine said.

'I see. I'm sorry to hear about this, but I don't see how we can help,' Claude said.

'I can see this is not a good time,' Sandra said.

As she stood there Claude didn't want to look at the reality of Sandra. Bertrand was Dredger's business. He watched her walk away, sadness embedded in her gait. Back in the house Maxine went to shower and Claude called Dredger.

'What is going on? His body turned up.'

'Don't know nothing about that,' Dredger said.

'You should. You were paid to get rid of him.'

'How do you know his body's been found?

'His ex-wife's asking questions.'

'What's she called?'

'Sandra.'

'Do you want me to get rid of her too?'

'No I do not.'

Claude hung up in anger and went upstairs where Maxine was stepping out of the shower.

He looked at her wet breasts and touched her. He took what he needed from her, what he'd paid Dredger for, and watched relief work its way across her face.

30

VLADIMIR ENJOYED THE SHOTS OF RINGER. HE FIGURED Dredger had done a good job. He was thinking of using him again. Dredger enjoyed Candy, she was a real class hooker. She did a few things he'd always wanted to ask a hooker to do and she did them well. When he got home to his flat he thought about Maxine.

Vladimir was sipping cognac in his office on Tuesday afternoon looking at the papers Spike had given him when Grigory walked in.

'Dat arsehole Dregger is no fucking good,' Grigory said.

'Vy?'

'He fuckin screw up da job. He vas seen.'

'Who by?'

'Fucking secretary, she came in for some papers, found door locked. Sat in her car and found Ringer and called an ambulance.'

'So he didn't kill him?'

'He shot him, but he's not dead.'

'You take care of him Grigory,' Vladimir said.

'Are dose da papers about Spike?'

'Dey are. Ve are going to take over his business interests.'

'And den?'

'Den you shoot him.'

'I shoot Dregger first.'

31

DREDGER STOOD OUTSIDE SANDRA'S HOUSE WATCHING THE windows. He'd start with her, then he'd get hold of Maxine. He had money now, he could buy them. He saw her at the window briefly, staring out at the street below. Then a few minutes later she came out and walked to her car. Dredger followed her all the way to Claude's house.

He watched her get out of her Audi and walk up the path to the house and ring the bell. When he saw Claude answer his head spun, she'd led him to Maxine. Then he saw Claude march her up the path and to her car. He had her by the arm and was talking to her in a loud voice, loud enough for Dredger to hear the sound but not the words. He got out, and walked up to them.

'Problem love?' he said, looking at Sandra.

'What?' Claude said, 'Mind your own business.'

'I'm minding yours,' Dredger said, amused by the pun. 'Now let her go.'

'Thank you,' Sandra said, walking away, back to the Audi, followed by Dredger.

He glanced over his shoulder at Claude who was standing on his path shaking his head.

'Are you hurt love?' Dredger said, using his softest tone, feeling gay as he did.

'No I'm all right, it's a little complicated.'

'It's about your husband isn't it?'

'How do you know?'

'I know what happened.'

#

When Claude went back into the house Maxine was in the hall.

'What was that all about?' she said.

'She's hassling you, so I got rid of her.'

'What did she say? You sound angry Claude.'

'Nothing much, she wanted to speak to you.'

Maxine put her arms around his neck and kissed him, feeling him grow hard against her stomach.

32

DREDGER AND SANDRA WENT TO THE FOX. HE BOUGHT A bottle of Pinot Grigio and watched her drink most of it, crying, asking him what he knew. He said enough to get him where he wanted, which was close enough to gain her trust. He told her he knew some bad guys had a grudge against Bertrand, described him in detail, the clothes he wore and that Claude knew something about it. Sandra began to beg him for details.

'I can show you a picture,' Dredger said.

'What picture?'

'Of Bertrand with these guys. I think he owed them money.'

'Money?'

'Gambling.'

'Bertrand gambling?'

'You'd be surprised how many wives don't know. Claude knows these guys, I was going to warn him off someone I know, someone he's pressuring when I saw you there.'

'I'm glad you came along,' she said, putting her hand on his arm.

'Another drink?'

'I shouldn't. I only started drinking like this since it all happened.'

'Why don't you tell me about it?' Dredger said, going to the bar.

And so she did, with tears in her eyes, about her marriage, about discovering Bertrand had seen other women and the news of his murder. She thought Dredger was a kind man, a little rough, not like anyone she'd ever known, but she was grateful for his help and now she felt she had something to go on.

'You mentioned a picture,' she said.

'Yeah, I've been following Claude, that's what I do.'

'You mean you're a PI?'

'Yeah.'

'Maybe you could work for me and find out what happened.'

'I'd be glad to. The picture is of Claude and Bertrand and the guys I mentioned.'

'Can I see it?'

'I'd need to get on a computer.'

'Do you have an office near here?'

'No, the other side of London.'

'I don't live far. Can you spare the time to show me?'

'Yeah, I think I can,' Dredger said, looking at his watch.

33

HE HAD A HARD ON AS HE FOLLOWED HER THERE, ALL THE way to the house he knew. He was thinking how it was a smart move, saying Claude was behind the killing, how he'd have Sandra and remove Claude, so he could get to Maxine. They parked and then walked up the path and she let him in. It was a real high sitting in her living room as she made coffee, talking to him like a regular house guest. He glanced at the pictures of Bertrand in frames, and talked to her about what he did for a living. He made it sound glamorous, protective. Then she got her laptop and opened it.

She was bending over it when he touched her. She was wearing a loose black dress and he ran his hand up her thigh, lifting it as he did and getting a good glimpse of her arse. She froze as his hand reached her panties. Then she turned round.

'Get out.'

'Come on, don't take on.' Dredger said.

'What are you doing in my house?'

'You invited me in, remember?'

'Now I'm asking you to leave.'

'I know things, I know what happened to him, how he was killed.'

'If you don't leave I'm going to call the police.'

'That would be silly.'

She moved past him and picked up the phone and Dredger grabbed her and pulled her onto the sofa. He didn't want it to be this way, but he needed to have her. He had one hand around her neck as he pulled her dress up with his other hand. Then he ripped her blouse open and pulled down her black bra. Her tits were as good as he'd imagined them to be, large and firm. He glanced down at her panties, not seeing the expression of horror on Sandra's face. Then he slid them down as she held her legs together. She was shaved and he liked that. He forced her thighs apart and unzipped his fly, then he was inside her, his face buried in her breasts.

When he finished he pulled away, a long strand of saliva stretching from his mouth to one of her nipples. He stood up and stared down at her. Sandra screamed. Then he realised what he had to do. He punched her, knocking her out. He went to his van, reversed it ono her drive, got some duct tape and his filleting knife. He gagged and tied her up, then cut away a section of carpet in the living room. He rolled her into it, then put her in the van and drove her to the boathouse where he killed her husband. He raped her several times before he finally shot her and weighted her down. Then he watched her sink into the Thames beneath a scabrous twilight that showed only the filth of the Thames, and Dredger's face reflected in it. As he drove away he felt something he was unable to identify. It was sadness, sadness that he had killed her and hadn't had the chance to show her how good they could be. But this was quickly displaced by anger. And it was anger that he'd helped Claude by removing her.

34

Cᴌᴀᴜᴅᴇ ᴡᴀᴛᴄʜᴇᴅ Mᴀxɪɴᴇ ᴡʜᴇɴ sʜᴇ ᴡᴀsɴ'ᴛ ʟᴏᴏᴋɪɴɢ, ʜᴇ watched her moods and the clothes she wore when she went out. He watched her as he made love to her, gently holding the violence in his soul away, as he caressed her slowly in the twilight of their room. He watched her as she spoke to other men. He watched her when she slept. And Bertrand's shadow stole into his house and adhered to the wallpaper that still smelt new and unbroken like the dream he'd found in the Bahamas. He wanted Maxine unviolated by the knowledge that Sandra presented, the lingering trace left of the dirty act he'd commissioned Dredger to carry out. He wanted Maxine's skin clear of blemishes and scars, those roots of the hidden past he'd left behind in the sunlit world where he found her. He wanted her, above all, he wanted her. He entered her hungrily with a beating heart. And in the morning light he saw lines and cracks on her surface, as if Sandra had changed something.

He considered Dredger's proposition, he thought if he had Sandra killed the threat would be over, but then there was Spike. He wanted Dredger out of the way, and so he called him.

'Decided to just take it on did you?' Claude said.

'Take what on?'

'Sandra, you asked me if I wanted you to get rid of her.'

'Did I?'

'You know you did. What were you doing outside my house?'

'Business.'

'What business?'

'You got something I want.'

Dredger hung up and Claude thought about it. He figured it was money. Maxine didn't seem affected by the news of Bertrand's death. In that there was some consolation.

35

Claude went to visit Al one rainy Sunday when it seemed the dawn was struggling to break all day. Claude told Maxine his brother was having money problems and there was no need for her to come along.

The morning he left, Maxine was standing in a pink G-string in the kitchen chewing on a corner of toast. The smell of the hot bread and her skin aroused Claude and he pulled the G-string down and slid his cock inside her. He wanted to consume her. He had his hands around her firm breasts, feeling her erect nipples as he listened to her panting and he looked into her eyes and wondered if it was all a masquerade, a trap for him.

He left the house and walked to his car, nodding at a man in a grey suit who sat in a Ford some houses way. Claude drove to Al's and looked at his brother's life, its emptiness, and he felt a surge of pride in Maxine as he gave Al a small amount of cash. Al was having money problems but that wasn't the reason Claude had gone there to see him.

'There's more if you need it,' Claude said. 'There's a lot more if you help me out.'

'I already told you.'

'But I need some muscle.'

'Who is it this time?'

'There's a guy, I asked him a favour, now he's putting me under pressure.'

'Who?'

'He's called Dredger.'

#

The man in the grey suit sat there watching the house all morning. At 11:00 AM Maxine left and got in a taxi. He tailed her all the way to Spike's house, watching the gates close. Shortly after, the taxi came out and the man waited. He timed her stay, just over an house in which she let Spike fuck her.

'I knew you'd be tasty, that time I touched your arse', Spike said, as he watched her dress.

'Can you get rid of Kathy?' Maxine said.

'Why would I want to do that?'

'Why do you think? Do you think I just sleep around?'

Maxine looked in the mirror, at the lines she saw creeping into her face on a daily basis. She wondered if Claude would lose interest in her one day and find another Caribbean beach and another woman. While Spike was in the shower she got a taxi and returned home an hour before Claude arrived, tailed all the way.

Claude and she drank some Burgundy as he talked about his visit to Al, how he was helping him out. He slipped his hand inside her blouse. Then in bed he saw the mark Spike had left on her skin, and he went into the bathroom where he bit his lip until it bled. He watched her shower, watched every inch of her naked dripping body as the soap slid off her.

Later he called the detective he'd hired. As he listened to the details of Maxine's visit, he clutched the phone with white knuckles, seeing Spike's face merge with Bertrand's and sink in a bleeding Thames.

36

Spike knew what he wanted from Maxine the first time he saw her and she let him hold his hand on her arse. The covert agreement was reached in the few seconds it took for him to establish that she would allow him to do that in the same room as Claude, and he knew it was only a matter of time before he slept with her.

Spike liked having different women he had no commitment to. He also liked having Kathy there. His loyalty to Claude was diminished by desire, and Spike desired other men's things. A few days after he slept with Maxine he invited her and Claude down, making sure the debt Claude owed him was paid in full. He also invited Vladimir and Grigory.

They sat outside in the garden and Spike tried to talk up his game, sensing Vladimir's wealth and needing to impress his guests. Claude watched it all with the measured scrutiny of a man plotting another's downfall. He wanted Spike removed and wondered where his desire for Maxine would lead him if she was a woman who gave herself to others. Vladimir bested Spike in money boasts. Claude enjoyed seeing him ousted by a man with danger written into his face and etched into the hard lines around his eyes which never sparkled when he smiled, as if he was merely baring his teeth.

And he saw Grigory watched too with a merciless look when Spike spoke. Kathy drank too much, showed too much leg, and Maxine behaved demurely, as if rehearsing the part of someone else. As Spike and Vladimir talked business Claude spoke to Grigory, who was smoking at the end of the garden.

'I have a job for you,' Claude said.

'A job.'

'There's someone I want to get rid of.'

Spike was visible through the glass doors, and Claude glanced at him as he said this. Grigory followed his line of vision.

'Call me,' he said, holding up his mobile phone, displaying his number.

Claude entered his number into his phone and went back inside.

Later, at home, he made love to Maxine. He searched for desire in her eyes and sated himself on her body. His sense of her arousal was broken when she said Spike's name. It was a whisper but he heard it beneath the groans. He heard it all night as she lay there next to him. And he ran his finger along the curve of her naked back as he thought of what he would commission Grigory to do.

37

GRIGORY SAT IN THE VOLVO WATCHING AS DREDGER LEFT his flat and got in his van. It was raining hard and pools of water formed by the London kerbs and settled in the pot holes, splashing passers-by as they walked down the narrow street. Grigory looked at the rundown building that housed Dredger's flat, and the petrol on the filthy tarmac, the bare trees and the grey sky and he thought of hookers wearing brightly coloured lingerie and performing for him on the money he'd get for killing this arsehole.

Dredger emerged wearing a pair of loose faded blue jeans, and a raincoat, walked fast to his van and drove away. Grigory tailed him for several miles to some disused garages, parking at the entrance, and waiting as Dredger got out and unlocked one. Dredger had just turned the light on when he heard a noise and turned. Grigory smashed him across the head with a blackjack. Then he pulled a Glock and shot him in the head twice, once in the ear then in the temple.

He drove straight to Vladimir's office, told him it was done, held out his hand for the cash. Vladimir gave him a look, Grigory knew what it meant, he didn't need to say, 'Step out of line and you don't work for me,' Grigory knew Vladimir had other guys he used, but not as good as him. Besides he knew more about him.

'Dat vas quick,' Vladimir said rising from his chair and opening the safe in the wall.

Grigory knew the combination, knew more than Vladimir knew he did, said nothing, took the 2 K and went back to The Marriott.

He spent the afternoon with two hookers, one white, one black, liking the combo. The black one gave better head, he made her get real dirty as he drank whisky. He gambled the rest away, staring at the Arabs in Crockfords casino, wanting one of them, wondering what their women were like beneath all the sheets. And he thought of Vladimir and whether he knew too much about him. He wondered if Vladimir would try to get rid of him. But he had his own ideas. And he wanted the kind of wealth Vladimir had.

38

SPIKE MET VLADIMIR AT HIS HOTEL SUITE THE FOLLOWING day. Vladimir had laid it on for Spike, the whole bit, the most expensive booze, a five grand bottle of Glenfiddich. He knew Spike liked single malt. He had some hookers laid on for later.

Spike looked through the papers and the files detailing the weapons, and nodded his head.

'You got a lot of money riding on this.'

'So ve do business,' Vladimir said, extending a hand.

'We do me old son.'

There was a glint in Spike's eyes, and it was a glint that Vladimir wanted to extinguish.

Spike handed him 100 K, sipped his whisky.

'Good drink?'

'Ain't bad.'

'Ve can make a lot of money,' Vladimir said.

'Guns is the way.'

'Ve pull dis deal off ve do a bigger vun. I have good outlets, you sell me da parts for good price, ve both make profit.'

'Name of the fucking game.'

'Ya, name of fucking game.'

Spike enjoyed the hookers Vladimir sent to the room next door. He liked the brunette with the big tits who unzipped his fly and took him in her mouth while the blonde stripped off. He had them both and left happy, returning to Kathy, who was drunk and lying by the pool.

While Spike had a swim, Vladimir met with Grigory.

'So how did it go?' Grigory said.

'Good. Ve have him and ve are gonna take all his money.'

'I tink Spike may not give it all so easy.'

'He give me 100 K, I'm going to pull him into a big deal den you can shoot him in the head.'

'Good I need da money.'

'Vat you do with the 2 K?'

'I spent.'

'You got a gambling problem.'

'Vat you think about Arabs?'

'Vat I tink? I tink dey're fucking pigs.'

'And da vomen?'

'Vat dey look like? I can't see da face.'

'Tink dey have hairy snatch?'

39

MAXINE TRIED BELIEVING CLAUDE HADN'T HEARD. SHE'D said it softly and she'd watched him afterwards as he lay there next to her. Claude didn't say anything to let on, acted the same, but she detected a subtle difference. She wondered if she was imagining it, but she knew he must have heard her say Spike's name as he was inside her. She thought he might not want to acknowledge it, might have made an excuse for her. She wondered how she could have been so careless and asked herself if Spike represented some appeal that was missing in her life. She thought of the two men, and of the different ways they touched her. And she wondered what she was, if not more than the recipient of their desires. She calculated her worth and she studied her body, looking for lines, feeling the firmness of her breasts.

She wished the episode with Spike away, fearing meeting him again beneath Claude's watchfulness. She knew he wouldn't get rid of Kathy. Letting him fuck her had been a pointless exercise, but one she enjoyed. She liked the way he touched her, liked the way he slid it inside her, he reminded her of the past, of occasional danger. She'd known men like him before. But Claude represented her future. And that was the problem, she figured, that morning as she showered, she was torn between the two. She'd had fun and been paid for, but now she wanted something more secure. She enjoyed Claude's company. As she looked out at the bathroom and realised he wasn't sitting in his customary position on the edge of the tub watching her, she felt hollowed and alone. She seemed to exist in a mirror of another's making.

#

Claude waited for news from Grigory. When Spike invited them round to lunch again he rang Grigory.

'When are you going to do it?' Claude said.

'I can't get to him.'

'What do you mean you can't get to him?'

'He's not an easy target.'

'I paid you for this.'

'I know, give me time.'

And so they went there, Claude watching Maxine all the way. And he wondered why Grigory was keeping Spike alive.

40

Spike made a good profit on his investment with Vladimir. Vladimir met him a few days later and gave him 150 K back on his 100. He put more in and waited.

Claude began to drink during the day, not much, a beer here and there, enough to push the thought of Spike inside Maxine away. He wanted him gone, the way Bertrand was gone, so he could forget. He hadn't heard from Sandra again, or Dredger. He thought about taking Maxine back to the Caribbean, even living there, and he finalised his plan to steal the painting. Yvonne called him on his mobile, asking what the delay was about.

'Complications,' was all he said.

Finding out about Maxine and Spike had sidetracked him and now he told himself to get the money and deal with it. It was clear Yvonne wanted it done soon, and so he decided to do it that Friday night. The problem was Maxine, what he would tell her. He wanted to do it late, but she'd suspect him of seeing another woman, and that might lead her to sleep with Spike again. According to the detective she had hadn't been back. And that was the way he wanted it.

He called Grigory again, asked him why the delay.

'I don't want to be found out.'

'I thought you were a pro.'

'I am.'

'Then do it this weekend, I want you to call me on Monday and tell me he's dead, all right?'

'Don't vorry I have a plan.'

'And what is that?'

'Juts leave it to me.'

'I've paid you half.'

The line went dead.

That Thursday Claude took Maxine out to lunch and thought of her and Spike, thought of Spike's hands on her and how in seeking his help he'd bought another rival. And he wondered about Maxine, wondered what he'd brought back from his holiday in the Caribbean.

As they ate Vladimir got access to Spike's bank details. He hacked in and sat back smiling. Grigory was watching over his shoulder, staring at Spike's assets.

'He fucking loaded,' Vladimir said.

Grigory drove to Spike's house.

'So Grigory what brings you here?' Spike said, one hand on the door, looking past him at the drive wondering where Vladimir was.

'I have interesting proposition to put to you.'

Spike took him through to the bar.

'Whisky right?'

'Right,' Grigory said.

He pulled the Glock from his coat pocket and fitted the muffler while Spike poured the drinks. When he turned holding two glasses Grigory shot him point blank in the head. Spike dropped the drinks and slid down the wall, a red smear on the wallpaper.

Grigory left, and drove back to Vladimir's office, calling Claude on his mobile as he did. Claude was having dessert as he took the call, said little, just smiled.

'It's done,' Grigory said.

'Good, thank you for telling me.'

'I vant da rest of da money.'

'Oh you'll get it all right.'

Back at The Marriott Vladimir glanced up from his laptop as Grigory walked in. He was looking at Spike's money, making plans for it.

'Dat vas quick,' he said.

'Shot him in his bar,' Grigory said, pouring himself a whisky.

41

With Spike lifted from him Claude felt back in the Caribbean again, just him and Maxine, sex and the night. The next day, after taking Maxine to lunch he removed her clothes standing in the hallway as he heard her whisper his name, her hand on his chest, his finger in the straps of her bra. He touched her breasts and pulled down her G-string. He wanted her more now Spike was gone.

He called Yvonne and told her he was doing the job that afternoon. She'd already told him she knew the owners would be out between 4:00 PM and 8:00 PM, giving him plenty of time to take it and leave.

'Call me when you've got it,' she said.

'If it's so easy why are you asking me to do it?'

'They know me, if I'm spotted on camera they'd identify me.'

'What about your fella?'

'They know Micky too, they're in business together.'

'Where are the cameras?'

'That's the problem, I don't know.'

'What do you mean you don't know?'

'The owner's a bit obsessed, he's got them hidden in the walls.'

#

Claude told Maxine he was going to see Al.

'He needs some more money, I shouldn't be late,' he said.

She kissed him in the hallway and watched him get in the Merc. He drove to Yvonne's address, a nice house in Kensington. She handed him the key at the door and he drove to Richmond.

He parked a few streets away, then put on his gloves and the jacket with a hood he'd bought that morning. He walked quickly to the house, got through the gates using the security code Yvonne had given him and walked up the drive keeping to the side to avoid triggering the sensor lights. He put on the balaclava outside the door, and pulled the key from his pocket. Then he was in. He found the alarm panel, entered the code and walked past the first door on the right, going into the next room. His Maglite showed him the painting where she told him it would be. Claude lifted it off the wall, slipped it in the large holdall and left the house, locking it and putting the alarm back on and closing the gates.

It was 8:00 PM when he handed it to Yvonne. She led him upstairs to an expensively decorated living room and inspected the painting.

'Good job,' she said.

'I better be off.'

'No drink?'

'Not tonight.'

'I beater get you your cash then.'

She handed him a large envelope and Claude counted it, then he left and drove back. He locked it in a drawer before Maxine came downstairs, then he kissed her and opened a bottle of Burgundy. They sat in the kitchen and drank it and he told her about Spike and watched her reaction.

'Shot, by who?' she said.

'If I knew that I'd tell the police.'

'Who told you?'

'Kathy.'

'Why would someone do that?'

'I think Spike was dealing with some dodgy people.'

Claude held her in his stare. He measured the emotion on her face, and he watched her face again that night as she lay beneath him and he entered her, searching for her desire.

42

CLAUDE MET GRIGORY THE NEXT DAY AT THE MARRIOT AND paid him. Grigory counted it out slowly in front of him, and Claude drove back to Fulham. Grigory sat drinking all morning, thinking about what he wanted. He was pleased with the fact that he'd been paid for carrying out what he knew Vladimir was going to ask him to do anyway. He'd delayed the hit long enough and kept Claude waiting. Vladimir hadn't paid him, but there would be cash. It was one of those jobs he just expected Grigory to do for him. And Grigory wanted that changed, he wanted cash each time he did one. He thought he'd hold onto the money. He was tired of killing and spending. He wanted to have the kind of wealth that bought him other pleasures.

That afternoon he watched as Vladimir seized Spike's assets. Transferred all his money to his Swiss bank account, sending it through other accounts to create a trail.

'Now ve have enough cash,' Vladimir said.

'For vat?' Grigory said, staring at the figures thinking jets, thinking guns.

'For vat I fucking vant.'

'More pussy?'

'Dere enough pussy here, something better.'

'Vat you gonna buy Vladimir?'

'You see.'

'Tell me.'

But Vladimir shook his head and sat down, ignoring Grigory's mood for the rest of the day.

#

When Claude got back from paying Grigory he felt he had her, Maxine, his holiday prize. He found her showering and he got in with her. She soaped up his erection, her eyes full of pleasure and the Caribbean, this woman of endless sexual adventure, his woman. He pushed the thoughts of other men away as she slid his cock inside her, and he pushed her taut buttocks against the glass panel of the shower. Afterwards as she squatted on the bidet he watched her wash her pussy.

'You don't need to do that,' Claude said.

'Does it bother you?'

'Leave it inside you.'

'It's hygiene.'

'Let's have children.'

She looked up at him and he was aware of the lie as soon as it had passed his lips and he felt afraid. He'd never wanted kids, he wanted her, only her and he wasn't going to share her, she could go on having men but he needed her body each night next to his like a reward finally, for all the years of trying to find a woman like her. She was his and she was a world of endless arousal.

'I can't have kids,' Maxine said.

'Why not?'

'I'm infertile.'

'It doesn't matter, Maxine.'

He watched her wash the rest of his seed away. As Maxine dressed she thought how two men she'd slept with since meeting Claude had both been killed. She became cautious around his watchfulness. She didn't sense any danger to her from him but she knew that her sexual appeal was as incendiary as paraffin. And she needed to be desired. She needed to feel the heat of man on her in the night. Her pleasures, many as they were, demanded appeasement. And she knew that her discretion would allow her the sexual luxuries she craved.

CLAUDE FELT MAXINE WAS CHANGING. IN BED SHE GAVE him more and he took it, wondering if the death of Spike was the motive. She seemed to be more interested in ensuring he was aroused, in exposing her body in the house at moments when he was least expecting it, as if her security lay in knowing she was wanted by him. She behaved as if she was addicted to physical contact, and he wondered if she was a nympho. He didn't mind, he liked it, liked the aching cock he woke with in the small hours as he rolled her over onto her side and slid it in, fondling her breasts as she slept. She came in her sleep sometimes and he'd press his ear to her mouth and listen for the sound of another man's name, hard as a rock, but she retained her silence and her wetness for him beneath his relentless sexual scrutiny.

She offered herself to him. She gave him that permanent erotic high, numbing him to any anger he might feel towards her for sleeping with Spike. She'd walk into the kitchen dressed only in a G-string, as she took a drink from the fridge. She'd pull her G-string down and take him in her mouth. Maxine feasted on his need, and dismissed the thoughts of Spike and Bertrand, the two empty memories that left her cold and alone in the night when Claude lay sleeping next to her. She knew she was an accoutrement whose identity was not of interest to Claude, who enjoyed men watching her, and she wondered how far his pleasure in this would go. She felt aroused if she knew that her price was rising.

Claude thought of moving with her. He wanted to remove her from other men's eyes, to have her to himself somewhere in the country maybe. With the money from the theft of Sweetie he could buy a place. And so one weekend he took Maxine house viewing in the Surrey countryside. He enjoyed it, walking around the houses, watching her talk design. They saw several places that day. But there was one house in particular that had what Claude was looking for. He could see himself fucking Maxine in each room. It was an isolated house surrounded by meadows. He wanted to take her there and make her his, really his, and gauge her desire alone with him.

KATHY DRANK HEAVILY FOR WEEKS AFTER SPIKE'S MURDER. She rang friends, rang the police, pestered them until they ignored her calls, and eventually asked Maxine and Claude to go round. Claude had called her the day after Grigory carried out the hit, spoken to her about Spike, saying how sorry he was. When Maxine called her and Kathy said she'd spoken to Claude Maxine thought Kathy had called him. Maxine told Claude they should go and see her.

Kathy was by the pool when they got there and rang the bell and got no answer. They walked round the building and went into the pool, Kathy getting up from a lounger, topless.

'Someone shot him, they won't tell me who,' she said.

Maxine took her arm.

'Let's go in the house.'

Kathy went upstairs and reappeared dressed a few minutes. They went through to the bar and she poured them drinks. Claude looked at the place where Grigory had done it. He couldn't see any stains. He wanted to get away from there.

'Who do you think did it?' Maxine said.

'I think it's to do with those Russians,' Kathy said.

'Why would they kill Spike?'

'Money.'

'I don't think they're short of money,' Claude said.

'There have been some weird things going on with Spike's account,' Kathy said.

'What things?' Maxine said.

'Money's going missing, being moved out of his accounts.'

45

GRIGORY WASN'T PICKING HIS PHONE UP. CLAUDE TRIED HIS number repeatedly, leaving no messages on his voicemail. Eventually he went round to The Marriott. Grigory opened the door to his room in a pair of boxer shorts, nothing else.

'I've been trying to get hold of you,' Claude said.

'Here I am.'

He walked back inside, Claude following him. There was a naked hooker on the bed and she got up and began to dress. She had huge tits, and Claude watched as she squeezed them into a blue bra, slid a thong on, then slipped into a tight leather skirt wiggling her hips to get inside, and put on a blouse and a pair of heels and left.

'You were going to kill Spike anyway weren't you?' Claude said.

'He didn't bother me.'

'Vladimir wanted him out of the way.'

'Did he?'

Claude saw the evasion in Grigory's eyes. Then he looked past him to the gleaming .45 Magnum sitting on the table next to a pack of condoms and a copy of

Hustler open at the centre fold, the model smiling distantly at the camera, her legs spread, ready for action, the muzzle of the gun pointing at her snatch.

'You took my cash for something that was going down anyway right?' Claude said.

'Vat you fucking saying?'

'Just that.'

'Fuck you, I popped dat cunt good, right dere in his bar, maybe I should have taken his bitch too, up da arse, where it belongs vit a slut like dat. Maybe I go back and tell her you pay me, take it to da cops, go back to Moscow for a vile, screw some Russian whores, dey better than de English slags.'

'I don't think you're going to do that.'

'You don't know vat I'm gonna do,' Grigory said, advancing on Claude as he retreated out of the door and began walking towards the lift.

He went home and found Maxine in the kitchen. She was wearing a sheer blouse and as he looked at the outline of her nipples he thought of the clothes in the wardrobe upstairs and all the times she'd worn them for him and he'd taken them off. Claude ran his hand up her skirt and between her legs, pulling her panties aside and sliding his finger inside her, his eyes locked on hers, seeking the evasion he'd seen in Grigory's face. He entered her on the counter, entered her on the table. And when he'd spent himself he looked into her eyes. He looked for the image of Spike there and saw Maxine stepping out of the Caribbean smiling like the whore in the Hustler magazine. He saw Grigory beating himself off, shedding his semen on her cunt as she drank vodka, he saw Spike sliding his cock inside her and he stayed locked in her as she gasped, locked there like a fox, shackled to the need and shackled to the hunger for her skin.

'Let's go away,' Claude said.

'Where to?'

'I want to buy that house in the country.'

'Oh yes, oh yes,' she said.

She felt him grow hard again deep inside her, as she dragged her nails across his back.

46

VLADIMIR PAID GRIGORY FOR THE NEXT HIT, THE ONE DREDGER messed up. Grigory sat in his Volvo running the notes through his fingers, 2 K more than he'd anticipated, wanting more. He found him in his house, sitting in a chair in his living room staring out at a lawn through a large window. His head was bandaged and there was a vacancy in his eyes. Grigory looked at him thinking he was shooting a vegetable. But Vladimir said reports indicated he would recover. And so Grigory unloaded the Magnum into his head, the sound muted by the muffler. It sounded like a sick cough in the quiet suburban area. Grigory walked back to his car and drove to Vladimir's office.

'I vant more for da next vun,' Grigory said.

'I pay you 8 K.'

'I know.'

'You better do vat you do to relax, Grigory.'

Grigory went back to the Marriott and paid for his two favourite hookers. He got them to strip and perform a routine as he sat in an armchair.

'Play vith each other,' he said.

The brunette stuck her finger in the black hooker's cunt and then licked her. Grigory walked over to them and fucked them both, taking his turn with each of them. He looked down at them, seeing Russia. When it was over he smashed them across the face, hard, but not hard enough to cause bruising. They started shouting and he grabbed the black one by the arm and threw her on the bed. He got the brunette by the throat.

'Here I pay you double,' he said, and tossed the cash on the bed.

Then he did them side by side, their legs parted, their hands locked around their ankles. Grigory licked the bruises on their bodies, smelling money and gun oil beneath their fabricated groans. He got them to kneel the way he'd made the thief in Russia kneel and beg him before he blew away most of his skull. Then he entered their open mouths with his cock. The black whore gave better head. He pulled on her head as he poured his come down the back of her throat and heard her choke.

47

ONE WEEKEND WHILE CLAUDE VISITED AL, MAXINE received a drunk and tearful call from Kathy.

'Those Russians killed Spike, I want them to do something,' she said.

'It might not be them,' Maxine said, thinking Claude, seeing Bertrand.

'Why are you saying that?'

'You don't know for sure.'

'Who else would have done it?'

'How much do you know about Spike's business partners?'

'I've met most of them.'

'What do you want done?'

'I want the police to talk to them.'

'Have you talked to the police?'

'Yes, and they've done nothing.'

'Do you think there's something about Spike you don't know?'

There was a silence on the other end of the line, a silence into which Maxine leant with all her fears of being found out by Claude.

'I know Spike screwed around,' Kathy said, 'I know he had other women.'

That was enough for Maxine. She drove round there, to make sure she wasn't under suspicion by Kathy, so that even if Claude had his doubts, they would never be confirmed about her.

When she got there Kathy was wandering around the house, a glass of cognac in her hand, her negligee open. Maxine saw a flash of pubic hair as Kathy sat down heavily in a chair and sipped her drink, her words slurred.

'It was here, he was shot here,' she said, waving an arm at the bar.

'I don't think Spike was of that much interest to Vladimir for him to get him killed.'

'Do you know why I put up with it? Spike screwing around?'

'Did he?'

'Oh yes, I knew about the other women.'

'Why did you put up with it?' Maxine said, keeping her eyes firmly on Kathy's.

'Because of this Maxine.'

She stood up and walked over to Maxine. She took Maxine's hands and placed them on her breasts. Maxine felt Kathy's nipples go hard. An hour later she found herself in Spike's bed again, Kathy next to her. It had been a while since she'd done it with another woman, and it felt good. And she realised that was what she was missing.

48

Maxine got back before Claude. She showered and changed. The image of her touching Kathy, her fingers inside her, the sound of Kathy's groans, the smell of her, her mouth on Maxine's, made her wonder what she was becoming in this avenue of suspicion and desire. She'd tried many things as a young woman, most of them on the light side of sex, but now as she considered being straight with Claude she felt afraid. She wanted a future with him, he didn't threaten her. She'd never hooked, not professionally, although money had exchanged hands in subtle ways and she'd known guys who used muscle on her, years ago, before the Caribbean. Claude was good to her and she liked him. She enjoyed the sex, although she sometimes wondered if it was really just something she did, like some women shopped. But then if Claude got Bertrand and Spike killed maybe he was dangerous. She didn't sense it with him, and she could sense a lot about a guy as soon as he began to fuck her. She thought about another life in the country with Claude, of endless sex on summer afternoons. And she thought about why she'd slept with Spike and her request he remove Kathy. And she knew the reason why. That day she felt she wanted more than Claude and Spike had it, Kathy was in the way. Now she told herself Claude was enough.

When Kathy put her tongue inside her she yielded for a moment to something else, something she hadn't planned on. It wasn't about control, but performance, and what was wrong in that? But Kathy had known how to touch her and she felt a deeper level of arousal than she'd known for years. She wanted more of it now, a woman's touch, she wanted Kathy to eat her pussy as she sat there waiting for Claude to return. The image of woman's tongue licking her tempted her to go upstairs and masturbate, something she never did. She'd wait for Claude and maybe unzip his fly as he entered the hallway, ask him to take her there on the floor, fill her with man. She poured herself a glass of Pinot Grigio.

When Claude returned she kissed him full on the mouth. She was in the kitchen and she knelt and took him in her mouth. And she thought of the body of the woman she'd touched a few hours ago.

'Take me away Claude,' she said, looking up, rubbing his cock.

'I'll take you somewhere we can have our own Caribbean.'

She slid his cock across her lips again and took him deep inside her mouth. Then she received the confirmation she needed and tasted her sense of control. She stripped then, shedding clothes in the kitchen, the hallway, and took him upstairs. And she got him hard again and guided him inside her and rode him until she came, knowing what she wanted.

49

THE POLICE PAID VLADIMIR AND GRIGORY A VISIT, TWO DUMB cops the Russians laughed at after they left. Vladimir and Grigory both had alibis on the day of Spike's murder.

'Dey're asking questions about the hit,' Grigory said when he rang Claude.

'Which one?'

'Spike.'

'Why now?'

'His vife is making trouble.'

'She's doing what any wife would do.'

'I don't give a shit about any vife. And dat drunken bitch is putting pressure on.'

'Kathy?'

'Yes, I'm going to take her out if you don't shut her de fuck up.'

'Why would she listen to me?'

'I may put a fucking bullet in her brain if she don't use it.'

#

As Claude took the call Maxine was with Kathy, watching her stumble around the empty house. She walked over to Maxine and fumbled with her blouse. Maxine watched with detached arousal as Kathy open her bra and she told herself that soon she and Claude would be away.

Her nipples were hard as Kathy touched them. The Kathy put her hand up Maxine's skirt, felt her wetness, sat her on a chair, parted her kegs and lowered her head. Maxine had been thinking about this ever since the first time, screwing Claude more and more to drive the desire for woman away. She lay back and let Kathy's tongue work its way inside her. Kathy was good, gentle, then increasing her rhythm. She felt Kathy's breasts, pulling them over the top of her pink bra, then she reached down and raised Kathy's skirt, pulled her G-string to one side, and put her finger inside her.

Claude was waiting for her when she got back.

'What were you doing at Kathy's?' he said.

'You followed me?'

'I went there to speak to her. I saw you leave.'

'Speak to her about what?'

'I think she may be making trouble for herself with those Russians. She thinks they killed Spike.'

'What if they did?'

'She doesn't want to get on the wrong side of them.'

50

CLAUDE HAD TOLD THE TRUTH. HE'D DRIVEN ROUND TO Kathy's and seen Maxine get in a cab as he pulled up. He sat there wondering if she was hiding something else from him, not thinking she was screwing Kathy. He'd stopped using the detective after Grigory shot Spike, and now he wondered whether he should put him back on the job. He wanted to know everything about Maxine, he didn't like surprises.

The day it happened Kathy was thinking of ringing Claude and telling him about her and Maxine. She liked Maxine a lot, thought they could live together.

She was in the hall when Vladimir and Grigory turned up. She opened the door, glass of cognac in her hand, and stood there looking at them thinking OK they've come to tell me, and I can finally know what happened and why.

'You better come in,' she said.

They followed her through to the bar, stood there looking at her, Vladimir with his arms crossed, Grigory with a tiny smile in the corner of his mouth.

'Was it you?' she said.

'Vas vat us?' Vladimir said.

'Who killed Spike.'

'Vat you tink ve here for?'

Grigory walked up behind the bar, Kathy stepping to one side, looking at him with outrage.

'What do you think you're doing?'

'Having drink.'

He poured a glass of Glenfiddich, dropped two ice cubes in with a pair of silver tongs and knocked it back.

'You come here and help yourself to my booze,' Kathy said.

'Sure, ve help ourselves to everything,' Grigory said.

'What else have you come here for?'

'Maybe dis.'

Grigory wiped his mouth on the back of his hand then swung it at her face, knocking Kathy against the bar, knocking her glass to the floor. Then he grabbed one of her breasts. Kathy tried to kick him but he got her on the floor, and pulled up her dress. He held her by the throat as he pulled down her panties.

'Look, bitch,' he said, opening his zip as Vladimir wandered around the house. 'I got a drink for you.'

Grigory enjoyed the outrage in Kathy's eyes as she entered her on the cold floor. He ripped her bra open with his free hand, all the while squeezing her throat hard enough to make her gasp but not too hard. He pushed deep inside her, seeing the hurt, and the humiliation as she tried to look away, but he took her face and made him watch his smile as he played with her tits, squeezing her nipples hard as he came. Then he pulled out and zipped up his trousers.

Kathy got to her feet. Grigory grabbed her arm and dragged her to the centre of the room as Vladimir came back in. Kathy was scared now, crying, and Grigory was enjoying it.

'Did you find it?' Grigory said.

'Ya I got da files.'

'What have you taken?' Kathy said, looking at the folder in Vladimir's hand.

'Rest of my assets.'

'Those are my husband's papers.'

'They're mine now, I've acquired his business, you're gonna have to leave dis house, maybe I set you up in a flat somewhere and you can get fucked by Russian tourists.'

'You fucking communists pricks, you should have stayed where you belong.'

'Vere is dat, Kathy vit big tits?' Vladimir said, walking towards her and fondling one of them as Kathy slapped him.

He laughed and grabbed her wrist.

'In Russia,' she said.

'Ve are Buying England, UK economy is propped up by Russian Mafia and Colombian cartel drug money, and de banks know it.'

'You're not taking my money.'

'I already have, you're just another vun of my whores.'

'Try her,' Grigory said.

'I don't fancy her snatch after you been in dere,' Vladimir said, putting the folder down.

'Open vide,' Grigory said, kicking Kathy's legs from her and grabbing her by the hair as Vladimir unzipped his fly.

She was eye level with his cock as she pulled it out and forced it in her mouth.

Grigory walked over to the papers Vladimir had set down on the arm of the chair where Kathy had licked Maxine. He leafed through the bank statements.

'Dis everything?' he said to Vladimir.

'Ya, dat's da lot Grig,' Vladimir said, moving Kathy's head backwards and forwards with his hands, which were cupped on either side of her ears.

It was an abbreviated version of Grigory's name Vladimir only ever used when he was experiencing sexual pleasure. They used to share whores in Russia and it had been a while since Vladimir has called him that.

Grigory set the papers down and walked over to Vladimir.

'I like dat,' he said.

'Vat, vatching me fuck whore's mouth?'

'No, you calling me Grig, like you used to.'

'You're not getting fucking sentimental are you?' Vladimir said, glancing at him.

'No, it just reminds me of ven I felt your partner.'

Vladimir looked away, down at Kathy's swinging tits below him and groaned.

'You coming?' Grigory said.

'Ya, suck bitch, suck harder.'

Grigory slapped Kathy's arse and then reached into the back of his belt. Vladimir was ejaculating into Kathy's mouth as Grigory blew his head off with the .45 Magnum. Kathy screamed, bit down on his cock, pulled away with blood on her lips, spitting come on the carpet. Vladimir fell to the floor. Then Grigory shot Kathy in the face and the side of the head.

'Vy?' Vladimir said, spittle and blood hanging from his mouth.

'Vladimir, Vladimir,' Grigory said, kneeling down, 'it could have been so beautiful, you and me partners, but you treated me like a second rate hit man, vich I am not.'

Grigory kissed him on the mouth, put his bleeding cock back in his trousers and zipped him up. Then he shot him under the chin, and left the house with the papers.

51

CLAUDE BOUGHT THE HOUSE IN THE COUNTRY, THE ONE surrounded by meadows. It was set in rolling hills and would provide them with the life they needed. He spent most of what he had left from the job and put the rest aside to do the place up. Claude drove Maxine there to have another look at it, talk colours and carpets. He stopped in a country lane on the way back and fucked her in the Merc.

'I've always wanted to do this, there's something about the smell of leather and your pussy,' he said.

Back in London he got Grigory's call, inviting them over to dinner at The Marriott.

'I don't think we can make it,' Claude said.

'Course you ca make it, by da vay dat bitch is dead.'

'Who, Kathy?'

'Somevun shot her, I don't vant people hearing about vat you hired me to do.'

'Why would they do that?'

'Dey von't if you come to lunch.'

Claude told Maxine about it as they sat drinking wine.

'He makes me nervous, I think he's undressing me with his eyes,' she said.

'He probably is, and who can blame him? I think we should go.'

'OK it's only lunch,' she said. 'But why do you think we should go?'

'He said someone's killed Kathy.'

'Kathy?' Maxine said, looking at Claude, thinking he had to know.

52

Yvonne called Claude the following morning.

'Got another job for you,' she said as soon as he answered.

'I don't think so.'

'What's the matter, lost your balls? You always did like to think you had a pair.'

'No, I don't want to go to prison.'

'This one's a beauty.'

'Yvonne, no.'

'I think you should speak to Micky.'

There was a pause while she handed the phone over to him. Then Claude heard a gruff cockney voice.

'Claude, pleased to talk to you, good job on Sweetie, how do you fancy coming into regular partnership with me?'

'I don't, like I just said.'

Claude hung up. He stared out of the window at the grey Fulham street as autumn settled in, leaves scattered everywhere, blowing along the pavement with the litter.

#

That afternoon they went to The Marriott. Claude felt nervous as he drove there.

'How come he doesn't have an address?' Maxine said as they got out of the car.

'I think these Russians like doing their business from hotels.'

'And why is that?'

'Because they're up to no good.'

'I hope this is the last time. I don't like him, I've known guys like him.'

'Yeah?' Claude said, looking at her, his brunette knockout in a violet skirt and matching jacket, all curves and expense.

'It was a long time ago,' Maxine said.

They went up in the lift. The door opened before they knocked, Grigory standing there looking smart in a designer shirt, Claude couldn't see what kind, and a pair of casual trousers. He looked at Maxine, his eyes on her cleavage that showed above the low cut top she wore under the jacket. Claude saw her fold her arms across her chest.

'I tought it be nice to see you after vat happened to Kathy,' Grigory said.

Claude nodded. They went in and sat in chairs opposite Grigory, Claude feeling the way he'd arranged the furniture was business-like. He wondered what he was going to ask of him and thought about the hit, thought about Kathy.

'No Vladimir?' Claude said.

Grigory shook his head.

'First Spike then Kathy,' Maxine said.

'Dere are a lot of bad people in dis city.'

'Spike must have left her a lot of money.'

'No good to her now.'

Grigory poured them a glass of wine each, a chilled Pinot Grigio from a bottle that sat waiting for them on a tray. He fixed himself a whisky and sat down again. Maxine kept her legs together as she sipped her wine.

'Who do you think killed them?' Maxine said.

Grigory shrugged.

'Vladimir dead.'

'What?'

'Shot, poof,' he said, pointing his finger at his temple, 'he vas getting blow job from Kathy at da time, somevun came in da house, blew dem avay and took papers.'

'What papers?'

'Who knows? Something to do vit money, let's eat.'

He got up and removed the silver plate covers from their lunch. They ate on trays, smoked salmon and salad, some nice cuts of ham and warm bread. All through lunch Claude felt they were being watched. Grigory spoke of his business interests and Claude waited for the moment he asked him to join him. But that moment never came. Instead Grigory started to say how much money he'd made in London. It seemed to Claude that Grigory wanted to assert his muscle. The knowledge of what he'd contracted him to do lay between them.

After lunch Maxine went to the toilet.

'I vant da interest,' Grigory said to Claude.

'What interest?'

'On da hit.'

'We agreed the price up front.'

'Ya, but dat vas before Vladimir got killed.'

'What's that got to do with it?'

Maxine came out of the toilet then and Grigory kept his eyes on Claude.

'I think we better get back,' Maxine said.

'Just remember dere is more dan vun vay of paying,' Grigory said, patting Maxine's arse at the door.

53

THE SECOND CALL CAME THE NEXT DAY.

'You better do this job,' Micky said to Claude.

'Or what?'

'Or I'll exert some muscle on ya.'

'Put me on to Yvonne.'

As he waited Claude thought about Grigory, of what he might do, thinking he'd killed Vladimir, taken Spike's money, and now he was after his. If he did the job then he could hire someone to take him out, but then if he got caught he was fucked. He couldn't have Maxine in jail. He thought of Grigory patting her arse with his heavy hand.

'Claude, what's the problem?' Yvonne said.

'I want to deal with you not him.'

'So you'll do it?'

'I'm not saying that.'

He met her later that day at a bar in the East End.

'I don't like your fella putting pressure on me,' Claude said as he ordered a beer, what he used to drink with her.

Yvonne was sipping a Campari and she swivelled on her stool, her skirt riding up her thigh.

'What if I did?'

'What if you did what?'

'Exert a little pressure on you, I always knew how to get you randy.'

'I got someone else, I don't want to screw you.

'Come on Claude, remember how good it was, my snatch, nice and wet, I always made you come buckets.'

'What would Micky think?'

'He wouldn't care, we have an arrangement.'

'Why me?'

'You're the best.'

'No,' Claude said, 'no more jobs, because it wouldn't end there, you'd always be after more.'

He rose from the stool and left the bar. Yvonne stared after him open-mouthed and made a call to Micky.

54

Claude visited Al first thing the next morning. He'd lain awake thinking about it, the pressure he was under from them, and made a decision. Al opened the door to his flat in Fulham in a dirty bathrobe, wandered into the kitchen and made coffee. The place was strewn with empty beer bottles and junk food. Al looked as though he hadn't shaved for days. He yawned, scratched his head and lifted a mug.

'Want one?'

'Yeah, I better,' Claude said, sitting down at the table.

'So what brings you here at eight o'clock?'

'Trouble, with a capital R.'

Al nodded wearily, made the coffee and sat down and waited.

'It's these Russians, they're pressuring me,' Claude said.

'Oh yeah?'

'I think they're Mafia, not top end, but heavy.'

'Russians?' Al said.

'Yeah.'

'How did you meet them?'

'Through Spike.'

'Fucking Spike, I might have known he was behind this. He got you put away remember?'

'I grew up with him.'

'Yeah, so did I. I don't see him though.'

'Anyway he's dead, so's his bird Kathy.'

'By who?'

55

'That's the bit I'm not sure about,' Claude said. 'He was shot at his house, now Kathy's been killed together with one of the Russians.'

'You must have a theory.'

'I got theory all right. Then there's Yvonne.'

'What's she after?'

'I did a job for her.'

'I don't believe this. You want to go back inside?'

'Her fella's pressuring me to do another one.'

'And who's her fella?'

'He's called Micky.'

'Yeah, I met him, and you know, he seemed familiar at the time. I know who he is, he's Micky the Butcher.'

'What's his real name?'

'Don't know. I seen him about, that's all, know his reputation.'

'What do you know about him?

'He's called the Butcher because he used to get people hurt bad, if they didn't do what he wanted. Knows heavies, knows a lot of them. There's a story about him hanging a geezer up at his meat factory in the

East End. He's an ex-pimp, turned fence for art thieves. That's why Yvonne's interested in you.'

'I told her I ain't doing it.'

'Bet she didn't like that.'

'No she didn't, but maybe Micky's changed his ways a bit, you said he used to get heavy.'

'You're kidding.'

'Al I need your help.'

'Russian Mafia, pimps, you're mixing with the wrong crowd.'

'Y OU MET MAXINE, AL,' CLAUDE SAID.

'Yeah.'

'This Russian bloke Grigory, he's threatening to do something to her. He ain't said nothing but he's making it obvious that he wants a piece of her if I don't pay him.'

'Do you owe him money?'

'No, but he did a job for me.'

'What job?'

'A hit.'

'This just gets better and better.'

'I paid him for it and now he's talking interest.'

'Who did you get taken out?'

'Spike.'

'Spike?'

'He screwed Maxine, I hired a detective.'

'You think he killed Kathy?'

'Yeah and his colleague Vladimir.'

'These fucking Russians are a bunch of cunts, and I don't like them coming here.'

'So you'll help me?'

'Yeah, I'll help you.'

THEY WENT INTO THE LIVING ROOM AND TALKED. CLAUDE looked at Al's boxing trophies for the middle weight titles he'd won. Al used to have real promise, Claude remembered how he'd put a boxer on his back with a lethal jab. Then he got into the crime, the stealing for drugs, and cage fighting, match fixing and his descent into a world Al did not want to return to.

'You were bloody good, mate,' Claude said.

'Still am, all right I'm overweight, I got the ability to take anyone down.'

'Ever miss it? The fights and the birds?'

'Na. You knew how it went down.'

'Look Al I'm sorry I'm involving you but who else can I go to?'

'Just your old bro, right. But Claude,' Al said, laying his heavy hand on his shoulder, 'make this the last time, I mean it. I'm not in shape, I can handle myself and I'll tackle them for ya, call in a few favours, but stay out of trouble, got it? These Russians can get real mean and I'll need a weapon.'

'Where you gonna get that from?'

'Remember Tony?'

'Tony who?'

'Yallow.'

'Course I fucking remember him, razor boy. Fucking killer.'

'Well, there you go, he's the man when you want a gun.'

'Is that right Al?'

Al nodded and picked up the phone. Later that afternoon he met Yallow at his well-appointed Surrey mansion, sat in the living room drinking tea from china cups while Yallow, a small man with eyes like a raptor, stared intently at Al, a boxer he used to enjoy watching in the ring. Yallow had tanned skin, tight muscles that ran up his arms, his right bicep showing a tattoo of the Marines, at odds with his white LaCoste T-shirt. Yallow spoke through sharp yellow teeth that made him look as though he was snarling.

'So Al, who is it you're gonna take out?'

'Some geezer named Grigory.'

'Grigory who works with Vladimir?'

'Worked.'

'How come?'

'Vladimir's dead, Grigory took him out.'

'Well, according to what I've heard these Russians hired someone to take out my mate Harry Simmons. He was my business partner and his death has not only left me in the lurch but caused me a lot of inconvenience, plus a mate's a mate and I always say if someone goes for your mates, kill the fuckers.'

'So you'll get me a gun?'

Yallow stood up and walked over to Al who sat with his finger stuck awkwardly in the handle of the tea cup.

'I'll get you one with no serial number, a good quality Beretta and I want you to hurt the cunt, right?'

'Got it.

'Now, any chance of you getting back in the ring?'

'Na, those days are gone.'

'Pity, you had one hell of a jab on ya,' Yallow said, faking a punch.

'Thanks Tony.'

'Who's this for Al?'

'My brother.'

'Claude was always getting into scrapes, still stealing?'

'I don't think so.'

'How come he's mixed up with these Russians?'

'Long story. But Micky the Butcher's also on the scene, shacked up with his ex.'

'Now that's a name I don't like hearing. What's he want from Claude?'

'He wants him to nick a painting.'

'Micky's trouble.'

'Don't I know it?'

'And he's shagging the lovely Yvonne?'

'Yeah.'

'Great pair of tits.'

'Yeah, so I heard.'

'Need a place to carry out the execution?'

'A place?'

'Yeah, where you gonna do it? Have you thought of that?'

'I thought I'd take him down on his patch.'

'Na, you do it at my lock up. Do them both, I mean there's no point leaving both the fuckers out there, right?'

'You mean pop Micky as well?'

'The way I see it is this. I want the man who got Harry killed dead, and the word is he already is, taken out by Grigory, you're saving me a hit man's fee by doing it. Now Micky has become a pain in the arse to a lot of people, me included, I had a painting stolen a while ago, and I think he's behind it, so take him out too.'

'Where's your lock up?'

'I'll show you, get them over there with a business proposition, call me when it's done and I'll dispose of them, remember my pies? Still got the factory.'

'Thanks Tony.'

'My pleasure, you know the Russians love them pies, fucking cunts.'

58

YALLOW TOOK AL TO A LOCK UP IN THE EAST END. HE GAVE him the Beretta, didn't ask for any cash, just said, 'Do a good job on those tossers.'

Al watched him drive away in his white Rolls Royce, then he drove back to his flat in his van. He looked at the Beretta, holding it in a tea towel. The handle was wrapped in electrician's tape. Yallow had given him a box of bullets. Al had killed before, in the army, and when he'd been involved in crime. He'd shot two men for threatening him, back in the days. As he was looking at the gun his mobile phone rang. He glanced at the caller ID and saw Claude's name.

'Micky's been round, so has Grigory,' Claude said when Al answered.

'What do you mean they've been round?'

'Just that, standing outside my door ringing the bell. I didn't let them in.'

'I got it, I'll deal with them.'

'Al, they're still out there. I'm looking out of the window and they're talking in Grigory's Volvo.'

#

Grigory had turned up while Al was with Yallow, and a few minutes later he heard Micky walk up behind him. Both men had come for what they considered theirs, Grigory for Claude's money or Maxine, Micky to make sure Claude did the job. Grigory had his back to Micky as he strode up the path in his cashmere coat. He turned when he caught a whiff of Micky's aftershave and both men stood there sizing each other up, with the instant recognition of two criminals.

'He in?' Micky said.

'I ring, no answer, but I tink he in dere.'

'What you want with him?

'Business.'

59

They were sitting in Grigory's Volvo outside Claude's house when Al turned up in his van, parked it a few cars away and thought about how to play this.

'Vat business are you in?' Grigory said to Micky, leaning across the seat, his arm on Micky's headrest.

'Art, I acquire and sell paintings.'

'Acvire, dat is a vord dat means you do it in a vay dat may not be legal, am I right?'

'Might be. You interested?'

'I'm alvays interested in business. How much do you make on a sale?'

'It ranges from 100 to half a mill.'

'Hm. You vant to meet me and talk about an idea I have?'

#

Al got out of the van and walked to the Volvo. He knocked on the door, driver's side, and saw Grigory swivel in his seat, glare at him and roll down the window.

'I think you want to speak to Claude.' Al said.

'Who da fuck are you?' Grigory said.

'I'm his brother, he told me he owes you a few quid.'

'Few quid, more dan dat.'

'Yeah well, he ain't got it but I do.'

'One hundred.'

'Sure, but I need twenty-four hours.'

'And you pay?'

'Yeah, if that's what he owes you.'

'It is.'

'Here's where you can meet me tomorrow, and I'll give you the cash then you leave him alone.'

Grigory shrugged, watched Al write the address of Yallow's lock up on a scrap of paper. As Al handed it to him, Micky leaned across the seat.

'Hello Al, long time no see.'

'Micky, what you doing here?'

'I just made a new business partner.'

'I thought you were here to see Claude.'

60

AL DROVE OFF, CALLING CLAUDE ON HIS MOBILE, TELLING him they should be gone soon, he'd sort it out. Meanwhile Grigory got out of his car and walked with Micky to his Bentley. He could see Yvonne inside, sitting there, her red varnished nails on the side of the door, her skirt riding up her thighs. Grigory looked at her fishnet stockings and turned to Micky.

'Come to my hotel tonight, ve can make deal,' he said.

'What sort of deal?'

'I know vere a lot of art is in dis country, rich Russians who collect paintings.'

'What cut do you want?'

'Ten percent.'

'That's reasonable.'

'Bring your vife, meet my vife too.'

'Yvonne?' Micky said glancing at her. 'She's sort of a business partner.'

'All da more reason to bring her.'

'Where you staying?'

'The Marriott.'

Grigory gave him the room number. They shook hands and Micky watched Grigory drive away, getting in the Bentley and telling Yvonne about the meeting then driving off.

'What about Claude?' she said.

'You're gonna go round there tomorrow and get him to do it.'

'And how am I gonna do that?'

'Fuck him.'

'I suggested it.'

'Do more than suggest it, get him in bed.'

As Grigory drove back he thought about the money he now had in his account thanks to Vladimir and Spike and the money he'd have tomorrow. Grigory figured Micky was after Claude's money, and he wasn't going to let him get it. He hated England, hated the people and the food. He wanted to return to Russia. He went back to his room and drank whisky and decided he'd have a party. If Claude's brother was messing him about he'd kill him, kill Claude, fuck Maxine and leave. And so Grigory celled up some hookers and booked a flight back to Moscow for the next night.

61

THE WOMEN ARRIVED AT ABOUT 7:00 PM. GRIGORY HIRED his two favourite whores, the black one and the blonde with the big tits. Grigory liked women with guns. He laid 50 K down and told them to strip, play with themselves, then he got out his Magnum and Glock, laid them on the table in the middle of the room, the women startled now, backing away.

'Pick up da guns,' Grigory said, 'use dem like dildo.'

The black hooker went first, picking up the Magnum, placing the muzzle against her pussy, rubbing it against her clit as she danced. Then the blonde picked up the Glock and began to masturbate with it, as Grigory thought of all the Russian whores he wanted to fuck back home.

He did some lines, letting the women snort, then he told them to go into the bathroom. They went in with the guns and Grigory took a bottle of Glenfiddich with him and a glass.

'Are these loaded?' the black hooker said.

'No.'

'You're seriously offering us 50 K?' the blonde said.

'Sure, but dere are a couple of tings I vant from you first, den I have dinner guests arriving.'

'You want us in the shower?' the blonde said.

'First bend over da tub, next to each other.'

Grigory watched the black whore lay her hands on the edge of the tub and the blonde get next to her and do the same. He unzipped his fly and entered the black hooker, her big tits swinging as he pumped her. Then he slid out and fucked the blonde, coming inside her and slapping her ass as he pulled out.

'OK now get in da shower,' Grigory said.

They climbed in and stood there as he took the Magnum from the side of the basin, swigged his whisky, and walked over to them.

'I fuck you vit dis, den you shower.'

'Then you pay us?' the blonde said.

Grigory nodded.

'From behind,' he said.

'Like this?' the black hooker said, turning and sticking her arse out at him.

'Good.'

The blonde one followed.

Grigory reached under the basin and slipped on the muffler. He put the Magnum against the black hooker's cunt and pulled the trigger. The blonde one began to scream and he punched her. He held her against the wall and shoved the muffler inside her pussy then shot her. Grigory drank the rest of the bottle as he watched them bleed to death in the bathtub.

Then he heard the knock on the door. He went into the hallway, checked himself in the mirror and changed his shirt.

'Thought you'd forgotten about us,' Micky said when Grigory opened the door.

'No,' Grigory said.

They walked into the room and he shut the door behind them then he shot Micky point blank in the face. Yvonne didn't get to scream because Grigory knocked her out with the butt of the gun. When she came to he was on top of her and inside her. She was naked and her mouth was gagged with her stockings and he was saying something to her.

'I don't like people muscling in on vat's mine. You should have been a hooker, after I fuck you I'm going to vash you.'

She turned her head away into the pool of blood on the carpet. Grigory pulled out and touched her, squeezing her nipples until tears ran down her face. He fucked her with the Magnum, pushing it as far as he could inside her. Then Grigory lifted her up by the hair and dragged her to the bathroom where he shot her.

62

GRIGORY BOOZED ALL NIGHT LONG, SNIFFED COKE, AND thought about what he'd do with the money in Russia. He left the Marriott with his case packed, and his passport in his pocket, placed the 'Do Not Disturb' sign on the door and drove to the lock up at 8:00AM. It was raining as he got out of his Volvo, stared at the slate grey sky and muttered, 'Give me a Russian whore any day,' as he pulled up the collar of his sports jacket and walked over to the lock up at the rear of the industrial area. He didn't see Al's van, which was parked around the corner behind some dustbins, he pushed the door open, found the light switch, turned it on and walked into the large area that was packed with boxes stacked from concrete floor to ceiling.

'Morning,' Al said.

He was standing right behind him as Grigory turned round. He hadn't seen him behind the door when he walked in, nor had he heard him make his way towards him on the rubber soles of his trainers. Al was pointing the Beretta at Grigory's head and he watched the scar that passed for a smile work its way across Grigory's face as he began to reach inside his coat for the Magnum.

'Vat you gonna do vit dat, let me show you real veapon, da vun I just popped dat Micky and his wore vith,' Grigory said.

All pulled the trigger twice, blowing the top of Grigory's head across the room. Grigory stumbled backwards into some boxes. Then Al stood over him and placed two more bullets in his head, one in the temple and one under the chin. He wiped the Beretta down on Grigory's jacket and dumped it on the floor next to him. Then he left him there, bleeding among the boxes, locked up and called Yallow on his mobile as he drove away.

'You got another pie,' Al said.

'Only one?'

'Grigory already took the pimp out.'

'I'll get rid of him.'

63

As Al drove back Yallow got in his Rolls Royce and went to the lock up. Behind the small office at the rear was an incinerator he used to dispose of his business rivals. And now, wearing leather gloves he put down some plastic sheeting and dragged Grigory across it, then dumped his body in the incinerator. He waited until it had burned down, as he sat and drank cognac at his desk and went through his mail. Then he took the Beretta, put it in a plastic bag, tied it up and drove to a deserted towpath some miles away where he went for a walk and dropped it in the Thames.

As he returned home Al was having a beer with Claude. He'd told him about it, how it went down, shooting Grigory and leaving him at the lock up. Claude sat there listening intently, enjoying the details, asking questions and then he gave his brother a bear hug. Al laid his hand on Claude's shoulder.

'I meant what I said, about this being the last time,' Al said.

'I know, and it will be.'

'Stay away from fucking Russians.'

'I ain't doing no more jobs neither.'

Maxine was in the bath as they talked, getting ready to go out with Claude and as Al was leaving she came down in a long black dress, her hair up, looking stunning.

'You joining us for dinner Al?' she said.

'Na, I had an early start.'

He left them and Claude took Maxine out to eat. Then he made love to her back at the house and heard the hiss of the Caribbean as he shut his eyes.

64

THE MAIDS WHO FOUND THE BODIES IN GRIGORY'S ROOM called the manager who called the police. The room was sealed off and a crime scene investigation area set up. The prostitutes both had records for soliciting and drugs charged and were identified. So were Micky and Yvonne. Micky had been inside for prostitution related charges, and Yvonne had a criminal record for theft and fencing stolen goods.

The hotel had a copy of Grigory's passport, but it didn't help the police, since he travelled under another name. They wrote it off as a Russian syndicate killing. Meanwhile a neighbour went round to visit Kathy and after ringing the bell wandered round to the pool. She saw the door was open and went inside, and found the bodies in the bar. The police investigated and identified Vladimir as a Russian gangster who'd been dealing in the UK.

They knew Spike's reputation and concluded that this was a UK gangland hit carried out in retaliation for Spike's murder. The fact that Kathy was naked and the wound to Vladimir's penis led to the theory that he had been having an affair with Spike's wife, taken him out and ended up ketchup on the wall as a result. Kathy's murder was put down to the fact that she'd obviously betrayed her husband, and his friends made sure she got taken out. They speculated as to which names might have been behind the hit, and came up with Harry Simmons. Spike had worked with Harry and they used to play golf together. But Simmons was dead. Yallow's name never came into the investigation. He'd been clever enough to keep his nose clean with the law for many years, always placing himself at a distance from any crimes he was involved with.

Dredger's name didn't come up either. His badly decomposed body was found some weeks later when a down and out went into his garage and reported what he found at the local police station. He was identified from his dental records as a hit man who the police were watching. No connections were formed between his murder and the other cases.

65

Claude and Maxine went back to the Caribbean for a holiday. He flew them there first class with the money he had left from the theft, and they stayed in the same room at the Raquel Boutique where he'd first made love to her all those months ago beneath an intoxicated sun. They sunbathed and went snorkelling and looked at each other beneath the masks they wore to see all the brightly coloured fish that swam away like sparkling coins in the deep blue water. Claude made love to Maxine feverishly beneath the cyanic sky.

He'd got rid of the men who'd been a threat to what he'd found out there, and he'd got her. And he never tired of her or ceased to desire her. They ate out at the places where they dined the time before and Claude thought of distant London and the rain. He thought of the Russians and Spike and how it all fell apart and came together.

He was retired, he told himself, and it was a retirement of sex and dining out. That wasn't a bad trade-off for the life he'd led before.

He wanted to buy Maxine things, he wanted to watch her put on the clothes he bought for her. Her body was a permanent erotic high.

'You ever mention Doris any more,' Claude said one evening as they drank chilled Pinot Grigio at Rio Mar.

'She belongs to the past Claude,' Maxine said, staring out at the sea.

'Something you want to tell me? You can out here and it will stay in the Caribbean.'

'She was an escort.'

'And you?'

'No, I did meet men who had wealth, but I don't do that any more.'

'How much money are we talking about?'

'Enough, Claude that's all I want.'

'So when I came along I must have been unusual for you.'

'No, I always liked your eyes. I didn't like a lot of the men I went with.'

'I used to wonder about you. I thought you were performing.'

'I like you in bed Claude.'

'There's no end to our pleasures now Maxine.'

'Now what?'

'Those Russians are gone.'

'There's something I want to ask you, but before you answer think about the fact that pleasure is partly illusion and partly trust, and the balance between the two is delicate.'

'Ask me what you want.'

'Do you know who killed Bertrand and Spike?'

'I know the killers were.'

'And you think it's best I don't know?'

'I think it is.'

'Thank you,' Maxine said, laying her hand on his arm.

66

BACK IN LONDON CLAUDE AND MAXINE GOT BUSY DOING up the house in the country. It felt good, free of Spike and Grigory. Claude didn't think about the other men, Maxine was his, the way he felt she was when they first met. And he'd managed to keep her. The sex just got better all the time.

On their first night in the house in the country Claude and Maxine ate at home in the large kitchen that stared out at verdant lawns. Maxine had got it done it up beautifully, tasteful pastel colours with a few paintings on the walls, abstracts mainly. She wore a low cut black dress and no panties, and Claude wanted her all through dinner.

They ate roast beef that Maxine had cooked and Claude looked at her seeing another side to her, thinking she'd never cooked for him. He liked taking her out, but he liked this too. They talked about the holiday and other places they wanted to go to. They talked about what they would do in the country.

Claude kept thinking of fucking her in all the rooms. He wanted to fuck her on the lawns at night while the village slept.

'We should have Al over,' Maxine said.

'Yeah we should, he'd like it.'

'I like your brother. I think he'd watch out for us.'

'I know what I want to do.'

'What do you want to do Claude?'

'I want to fuck you in every room and on our grounds.

'It would be a shame not to.'

'Why don't we start tonight?'

'I think I'm dressed right aren't I?' Maxine said, standing up.

'You're dressed just fine.'

'You know two things get people killed, sex and money.'

She walked over to him and raised the hem of her dress, then she undid his shirt and unzipped him and sat on his lap. Claude put his arms around her neck as she guided him inside her all the way home. He looked into her deep brown eyes and saw his own reflection there. Maxine began to moan, the way he liked it.

'It's not just about sex is it?' Claude said.

'Not with you baby.'

She continued moving, and he was locked there inside her, deep between her toned tanned thighs. She moved him all the way to his high, the one he knew so well. And as he emptied himself inside her he felt her twitch and come and she leaned over and bit him gently on the shoulder. And he kissed her mouth and tasted himself on her lips, tasted the erotic sea and all the things he knew she could do as she pulled the dress all the way over her head.

www.ingramcontent.com/pod-product-compliance
Lightning Source LLC
Chambersburg PA
CBHW022049050726
47591CB00002B/461